The Sand Witch

Other Avon Camelot Books by
Steve Senn

THE DOUBLE DISAPPEARANCE OF WALTER FOZBEK

RALPH FOZBEK AND THE AMAZING
BLACK HOLE PATROL

STEVE SENN was born in Americus, Georgia, and grew up in a small southern town whose main industry was producing peanut butter. He attended Ringling School of Art in Sarasota, Florida, and presently lives in Jacksonville, Florida, where he works as an art director. He also paints pictures and writes books, including two previous Avon Camelot titles.

The Sand Witch

Written and Illustrated by

Steve Senn

AN AVON CAMELOT BOOK

THE SAND WITCH is an original publication of Avon Books. This work has never before appeared in book form.

AVON BOOKS
A division of
The Hearst Corporation
105 Madison Avenue
New York, New York 10016

Text and illustrations copyright © 1987 by Steve Senn
Published by arrangement with the author
Library of Congress Catalog Card Number: 87-970
ISBN: 0-380-75298-0
RL: 5.4

Library of Congress Cataloging in Publication Data:

Senn, Steve.
  The Sand Witch.

  (An Avon Camelot book)
  Summary: On vacation at the beach, Frick and Jenny help a witch from outer space search for a giant candy-eating crab.
  [1. Extraterrestrial beings—Fiction. 2. Witches—Fiction. 3. Beaches—Fiction] I. Title.
PZ7.S474San   1987   [Fic]   87-970

First Camelot Printing: June 1987

CAMELOT TRADEMARK REG. U.S. PAT. OFF. AND IN OTHER COUNTRIES, MARCA REGISTRADA, HECHO EN U.S.A.

Printed in the U.S.A.

OPM   10   9   8   7   6   5   4   3   2

Contents

Stre Senn

The Sand Witch

1: Things Go Bump in the Night

"LOOK! A shooting star!" Frick said.

It was a long one, too. It lasted maybe three or four seconds and went from the top of the windshield to behind the farthest row of trees ahead.

"Wow," I said, as if it was a big deal.

"Another point!" Dad said, delighted. "That makes three meteors you've spotted since we left Prentiss, Frick." Then he turned to me. "And only one for you, Jenny."

I shrugged. I was going to lose the game anyhow. We only had a little way to go before we reached Cobweb Cove and the meteor-counting game ended. But I was still kind of jealous Frick had been the one to record such a sparkler.

When we travel at night we play the meteor-counting game. It helps to pass the time, and Dad always gives the winner a comic book or something. Our dad is into astronomy. Frick and I were squished together with our chins on the back of the front seat because most of the back of the car was filled up with Dad's eight-inch Newtonian telescope (plus luggage). The telescope is Dad's pride and joy, so we try not to complain. Mom gets to ride up front with the ice chest, so she doesn't care how much space the telescope takes.

"That meteor came from the direction of Hydra," Dad said, showing off.

Frick whispered to me, "Did that one look kind of funny to you, Jenny?"

Frick is short for Frederick, and he's my kid brother. He's only seven, three years younger than me, but he's smart for his age. Somehow, he's usually ahead of everyone else. Precocious, Mom calls him. That's adultese for having a wise mouth.

I shook my head. But, as a matter of fact, that last meteor *had* looked strange. It never went out, it just disappeared behind the trees. But we were getting close to town and I didn't want to think about the meteor anymore. I wanted to think about the beach. I tried to smell the ocean, but all I could get was Frick's peanut-butter breath.

Cobweb Cove is wonderful. It's a sleepy old fishing village with weathered homes and fishermen dozing on rickety docks. We go there every spring vacation for a week. Its real name is Cobb's Cove, but we think cobweb fits it better. Sounds scary, now. It sure got that way this trip.

"We're here!" Frick chimed when we passed the city limits sign.

It gave me a thrill to see the little town, too, after a year. Even in the dead of night. Small towns look so deserted after dark. The only face I could see as we drove through was on the huge statue of King Neptune that stands in front of the courthouse.

Soon we were rattling over the wooden bridge onto Summer Island. There are lots of rental cottages like ours on the island, though most are fancier. We could see their lights winking through the trees. Frick thought every side road was ours. He kept squealing that Dad had missed the turn.

"Shut *up!*" I elbowed him, missed, and paralyzed my funny bone on the door. But I was eager to reach the cottage, too. I could smell the ocean for sure, now.

"Hey, look," Frick said. He stopped squealing. "There's a new house on the salt pond. Weird. It looks like it's been there forever."

The salt pond was right next to our cottage. And Frick was right. I could see just the silhouette of a funny little antique house there on pilings, with lots of fancy railings and shutters. It had one light on, and looked very eerie when you realized there wasn't supposed to be a house there. At the time I didn't pay much attention to the cloud of fog around it. Somehow, the house made me shiver.

"Look, Sam" Mom said to Dad. "Frederick's right."

Dad glanced at the new house and snorted. "Somebody must have a load of money. Imagine what it cost to transport that from whatever old town it came from to Summer Island instead of just building here."

Then he and Mom started talking about how Uncle Henry moved his house from Palmsboro, and then about how much construction costs these days, and forgot about the house. Grown-ups are like that.

Alice says adults have to see things very humdrum and logical. That way they can stay calm enough to go to work and stuff. They never notice what kids notice, and when they do they don't see them the same way. Alice's Law, she calls it. Alice is my best friend back in Prentiss. She wasn't with us or anything on our spring vacation. I only mention her because I thought about her law all that week.

When I finally looked away from the new house there was our beat-up old cottage in the headlights. The car stopped. Frick whooped and crushed my foot as he bounded out of the car. Then I whooped and limped after him.

The cottage was in pretty bad shape. The wind banged the screen door against the wall. It was nearly off its hinges, and the screen was out. There were beer cans all around the steps.

"Snerk!" Dad said (he hates to curse in front of us so he makes up his own words). "I wish people would have the decency to leave the snicking cottage in good shape when they go! Frap! Just look at that, and me with no tools!"

"Now, Sam," Mom said. "We can pick up a hammer and some nails when we go into town tomorrow."

The cottage was dark and empty. It smelled like other people. With the mysterious appearance of the house next door and the hollow sound of the door banging in the wind, I began dreading the first night there. Frick felt the same way. I could tell by the look he gave me. Then I stamped on his foot in revenge and ran outside to help with the luggage.

Mom is great. She had the place homey in no time. She dusted and opened the windows and got the tackiest paintings off the walls. Lots of people rent the cottage during the year, but Mom has a way of turning it into our own private beach house.

It was late by now. After we had unpacked I got to take the first bath in the old yellowing bathtub. It's more fun than taking a shower. It has feet and a tall swoop back that you can lean against.

Afterward, I tried to talk Dad into letting me run down to the beach for just a peek at the surf, but it was no use. To bed it was. I slid between the crisp folded sheets Mom had just put on the bed and watched the little yellow light of the new house wink across the salt pond through the window beside my bed. Frick finally thumped out of the bathroom with his pajamas still sticking to him because he doesn't dry off very good. He got in the other bed. Lights out.

After a while the lights in the other part of the cottage went out. All I could think of was hitting that beach tomorrow. Sleep seemed a long way off.

"Jenny?" Frick whispered.

"What?"

"Is the new old house still there?"

"Of course it is," I said. "Did you think it flew off while you were bathing?"

There was a long silence as if he wasn't sure what he thought. "I dunno," he said. "But it sure looks weird. Maybe a wizard lives there. Or even a witch. Let's go over and explore tomorrow."

"Sure," I said. But I was thinking of wonderful waves.

He wanted to talk a bunch more. But after a while with me answering "yes" or "no" or "maybe" to everything, he fell asleep.

I closed my eyes and tried not to think about how much fun it would be playing in the surf in the morning. It was pretty difficult since I could hear the roar of waves just down the beach. But after a while the sound soothed the thoughts right out of me. I was drifting into a nice soft sleep on invisible waves. . . .

Rain? I tried to ignore the sound of a sudden shower approaching my window across the dunes. The drops spattered across the sand. Sometimes it rains suddenly at the beach.

Then . . . BUMP! I sat straight up. I think my heart hit the roof of my mouth. Frick peeked over his covers.

Something had hit the roof. Overhead, a dragging noise slid over the shingles. It went from one end of the house to the other. Then there was only the sound of the rain. Then it stopped, too.

Boy, was there silence then. Even the crickets had shut up.

Frick's gulp sounded like someone stepping on a frog. "What was that?"

Trying to sound adult, I said, "Just the wind. Probably knocked the front door the rest of the way off." But we both knew I was lying. The sound had come from above.

We finally settled down, but my ears felt like radar

dishes. I swear I heard every cricket and every gust of wind. Not to mention every bump of the door.

I faced away from the new house next door. My heart was going like a drum, and it didn't calm down until a lot later. Then, somehow, I got to sleep.

2: I Hate a Mystery

I woke up in a fog. I couldn't remember falling asleep, just lying awake listening to my heartbeat. Then I remembered where we were.

"Whoopee! The beach! Let's go!" I said.

But before my feet hit the floor I was stopped by the expression on Frick's face. He was just sitting in the middle of his bed, in a sunbeam, looking down at something.

"What's that?" I said, peeking over his shoulder.

He seemed to notice me for the first time. "Oh, hi, Jenny," he said. "You just now getting up? I've been up for hours—I don't know how you stayed asleep so long. We're at the beach!"

It was a little chunk of metal, flat and yellowish, with curls and spirals sticking out of it, and it had made dirty marks over Mom's sheets. I grabbed for it, but he pulled it away jealously.

"Hey, where'd you get that?" I wondered.

"The fireplace, in the ashes," Frick said while he held the thing up and squinted out the window through a spiral.

"Yeah," I smirked, "and you got soot all over your bed."

"It's magic," he said confidently.

"What are you talking about? You're weird, Frick."

"Whatever bumped into our house last night dropped it down the chimney. I think it's a spell, Jenny."

Just then Dad pounded on our door for us to come to breakfast or starve, or I would have told Frick how weird he was again. A spell? I would have laughed, but the smell

8

of bacon had me under its own spell, and I jumped into my clothes.

After I'd had a glass and a half of orange juice and enough food to wake me up I waited for a break in the conversation and mentioned the funny noise last night.

"Mmff?" Dad said sleepily, trying to find his face with the coffee. "Sound? I didn't hear anything. Did you, hon?"

Mom smirked. "Just your snoring, darling."

"I don't snore," Dad grumped.

"Then there's an alligator hiding in our bedroom," she replied

No, they didn't hear any noise. And when I described it, Dad, true to Alice's Law, said it was "just the house settling." But before I could try to reason with Dad, Frick jumped in.

"If it was just the house settling, who dropped this magic medal down our chimney?" He held up his prize defiantly.

Dad laughed real loud at that. "Looks like just an old piece of fireplace grating, Frick. Sorry, but I don't think there's much magic in that." He winked at Mom, and I could tell they thought Frick was being precocious.

Frick put the thing back in his pocket with a funny, smug look on his face. I didn't think it was magic, but Alice's Law made me suspect Dad's explanation, too. It didn't look like any fireplace grating I'd ever seen. But I wasn't interested in mysteries right then. I just wanted to finish my breakfast, forget about strange sounds and magic medals, and get outside.

Sunlight on waves sure is nice. Frick and I ran down to the beach and just wiggled sand between our toes. I had been waiting for this all winter. I kicked some shells around, then spent some time chasing the waves out and being chased back in by them. There were birds and crabs to chase, too. I couldn't wait to get my swimsuit on and hit the surf, but of course Mom wouldn't let us swim right after eating so we wouldn't swell up and drown, or something. Besides, we were supposed to go into town with her to get groceries.

One of the bad things about having a kid brother is you are expected to keep an eye on him. I had both eyes on a neat spotted crab hiding in some seaweed before I realized I didn't know where Frick was.

"Frick!" I called. Some old ladies collecting shells looked at me like I had lost my mind. I explained what a Frick was and they pointed to a tall dune behind me. Frick was on top of it looking toward the salt pond.

He noticed me coming to get him and said, "Come on, you can see the new old house good from up here."

You could, too. It was out on the end of its own little pier in the middle of the salt pond, which was behind the dunes. The pond fills up at high tide and almost empties at low tide. Now it was low. The house looked deserted, and even more haunted than it had last night.

"Isn't it strange?" he bubbled.

"No," I said to discourage him. "C'mon, let's go play in the surf before we have to go to town."

I was halfway down the dune when I noticed Frick hadn't moved. He was looking at the ground.

"Hey, Jenny! Did you know octopuses could climb dunes?"

"Frick," I said, "did you know seven year olds could fly? I'm gonna come up there and make you fly off this dune!"

Then I noticed what he was looking at. There were long tracks in the sand, going up and coming down the dune, where something heavy had passed. All along the tracks were lots of donut-shaped things.

"Suckers," Frick said scientifically. "And they're coming from the new old house."

A chill went through me. "You're the only sucker that's

been on this hill lately," I said, swatting him down to the water.

Later, when we piled into the car to go to town, Frick wasn't as bouncy as he usually is. I had tried to explain that octopuses don't come out of the water, but I couldn't explain those strange prints. Frick wasn't scared or anything, just kind of thoughtful, and he kept his hand in his pocket where the weird medal was.

I tried not to worry about him or wonder about mysteries. I just wanted to enjoy this vacation.

Cobweb Cove was really bustling. There were maybe twenty people downtown shopping. Twenty people would make Prentiss look deserted, but here they nearly clogged the narrow street that circles the courthouse. Most of the shops are on that circle. The courthouse is a big brick castle with turrets and a giant clock, and on its front lawn the statue of King Neptune, almost as big as the courthouse itself. He's a giant bronze statue leaning on his trident (that's a kind of fisherman's pitchfork) with all kinds of seafood spilling out of a shell in his other hand. There are metal lobsters and oysters and shrimp all spilling down the base nearly to the grass, and a fountain sprays water over them all. I like to think it's salt water, but it probably isn't.

Dad went off to the docks to talk to some friends he'd made over the years we'd come to Cobweb Cove, and Frick and Mom and I bought what groceries we would need for the week. We always do that, instead of bringing everything. Then Mom remembered promising to pick up some tools for Dad.

Mr. Poole, owner of Poole's Hardware, grinned at us when we came into his store. "Welcome! I guess it must be spring holidays again."

"Goodness!" Mom said. "What happened here?"

Mr. Poole was sweeping up a pile of broken glass. He had the shop door propped open so no one would hurt himself on its shattered window. He leaned forward on his broom, his brow wrinkling all the way up his bald head when he frowned.

"Punks," he said. "Must have been a couple of rotten apples from Neptune High. Nothing serious, luckily. They only took a couple cans of copper spray paint—to write their names on a wall, I guess. You know what they say: 'Fools' names like fools' faces are often seen in public places.' Anyway, I got off pretty good. Hall's Dime Store next door lost a whole box of chocolate kisses. They smashed the whole candy counter."

Mom looked shocked. I didn't. A lot worse stuff than that goes on in Prentiss all the time. But I like Mr. Poole, and I was sorry his store got broken into.

"Say, kids," said Mr. Poole, when Mom had gone looking for a hammer. "How would you like to win fifty smackers?"

"You mean dollars?" I said. Frick didn't say anything. I guessed he was just being mysterious. "Sure!" I said quickly. There was a lot I could buy with half of fifty dollars.

"Well, you know the annual Crab Trap Festival is at the end of this week," he said. "And I usually have a float in it, but this year I've been too busy to fix up one. Would you two like to build me a Poole's Hardware float and drive it in the parade?"

"Sure!" I gulped.

"Dandy!" he said. "I remember what a fine job you kids did in the sand castle contest, and your solar science project you built last year. I've got an old riding lawn mower you can build the float on and some materials. There's a fifty dollar prize for Most Original Float, and I bet you kids could come up with a winner."

"Neat!" I said, trying to make up for Frick's quietness. The thought of that Most Original prize was tempting. The most original thing I'd seen at last year's parade was a shrimp boat engine painted green, drawn by a pickup truck.

By the time Mom got back with the hammer and stuff we had settled all the details. Thoughts of the prize money were swirling in my head. I don't know what was swirling in Frick's head. He still wore that distant look. I had to give him a little nudge to get him out the door.

Frick heard the noise first. He must have. The first thing I remember is seeing the hair on the back of his head all rise up like a frightened cat's. He turned and grabbed my arm.

"PopPopPopPopPopPopPopPopPopPopPop," right down the street.

I followed Frick's gaze and there she was. "It's the witch next door," Frick whispered.

She stopped her bicycle and smiled. It was a weird smile, like her face was winking. I gulped. Both tires were covered with suckers. That was what had made the marks on the beach and the funny noise just now. She had tiny pale eyes, a squarish body, and long boney arms and legs. She was wearing a pair of fuzzy bedroom slippers and the plainest dress I've ever seen. More of a bag, really.

"Stop staring, children," Mom said, trying to hurry us along.

"She lives in the new old house." Frick pointed at her, and the witch stared right at the tip of his finger, still smiling, as though she had never seen a fingerprint.

Mom was embarrassed. She introduced us.

The witch smiled even wider and her bumpy cheeks bunched up. She held out her long hand so we felt obliged to shake it, which I didn't like at all. My hair must have risen, too. There was pink webbing between her fingers. I didn't want to think about what her slippers were hiding.

"My name's Wanda," she said in a calm voice. "I'm so happy we're neighbors. Perhaps you can come and visit me sometime. I have cookies and tea to share."

All I could think of was Hansel and Gretel and the sweet

old lady in the gingerbread house. Mom returned her greetings and we went to find Dad, with Wanda's pale eyes staring right after us.

"What a nice old granny," Mom said. I shuddered.

When we got back from town, we finally got into the water. I think the only time Frick and I were out of the waves the rest of the day was right after lunch, while we waited for the bloating to go out of our muscles. The waves picked us up and tossed up back to shore maybe a million times. Frick stepped on a crab and nearly freaked out. I never knew he could jump so high. He almost hit a seagull.

By the time Dad came and got us we could hardly see each other, it was so dark. We bathed and ate supper, but we had been in the water so long it still seemed like the waves were moving us back and forth. And all our toes and fingers were wrinkly from the water. I love that.

There was a show on TV about spies, but what I remember most about that night was what we saw after we went to bed. At least I had gone to bed. But I heard a noise and rolled over to see Frick looking out my window.

"There she is," he said when he noticed me. "She's not flying tonight."

You could just see her in the moonlight, over the dunes. She was wandering through the tall sea oats and appeared to be looking for something. She was singing a peculiar sounding song in a high voice. There was a dog or something on a leash (it was the "or something" that bothered me) and it was raising big clouds of sand. The sand whipped around her all white in the moonlight, like it was glowing.

Frick gave her her name then and there.

"The Sand Witch," he whispered in awe.

3: The Whale Tale

THE next morning I really thought things were back to normal. The sun lit up our room early, letting us know the beach was ready. Frick seemed as eager as me to wriggle into a swimsuit and get to the water. He didn't mention the Sand Witch. I was grateful for that. I was ready to forget the whole spooky subject and get on with our vacation.

But when we bounded toward the door there was Dad, loaded down with fishing rods and nets and grinning from ear to ear.

"Well," he hooted, "ready to hit the bounding main? Batten down the hatches and secure the mizzenmast!"

It's sad when a grown-up goes crazy. Frick and I exchanged pitying glances and tried to creep around him.

"Come on!" Dad cried. "Aren't you ready for our deep-sea expedition on the *Neptune Queen?*"

I flinched when I remembered him telling us about the *Neptune Queen* on the way back from town yesterday. That's what he had been doing at the docks—booking us to go deep-sea fishing. I had only been half listening because the Sand Witch's pale eyes and webbed fingers and bizarre bicycle had been still churning around in my head. I barely remembered the plans for the all-day fishing trip.

Frick and I whined and muttered. We would much rather be on the beach than on a boat all day. But we could tell by the deepening purple color of Dad's nose that there would be a major explosion if we made him go alone. Also, his bottom lip was sticking out farther and farther, a deadly

15

sign. We agreed to go when we found out we didn't have to put anything alive on our hooks.

"They furnish squid pieces and chunks of mullet," Dad soothed.

"If it's so easy why isn't Mom going?" Frick grumped.

"Seasick," came her reply from behind a magazine. "When I get on a boat I get deathly ill and throw up my shoes. Can't even look at a boat. Ask your father what happened when he took me to see *Moby Dick* at the drive-in."

Dad blackened. "She ruined the upholstery in my Dodge."

That let Mom off the hook, but Dad made a lot of snide remarks about her delicate digestion that he was very sorry about later.

The *Neptune Queen* was a huge double-decker boat with green paint peeling off all over it. It had one of those wooden statues on the front for good luck, but I don't think it worked very well because most of the figure had been ripped off in some accident. Only half a mermaid was left. The boat was crowded with a lot of men drinking beer and smoking terrible cigars. Most of their wives must have been smart enough to have delicate digestions too. The boat throbbed when the captain started the engines. I never knew diesel engines smelled so bad.

Frick and I were disgusted. We were going to have to stay on this awful boat the rest of the day. I began to regret promising to make that float for Mr. Poole. I might never have time to get back to the beach.

Dad was excited, though. We seldom see him that keyed up. He tried to drop a line right over the side in the harbor, but everyone laughed at him, and he turned purple again and put his rod up. It turned out he didn't even have to bring all that stuff anyway. They supplied everyone with rods and electric reels and bucketsful of squid arms for bait. In case you've never seen squid arms, they look like the palest worms in the world and feel like rubber bands that have been in the sun too long. Even the flies left them alone. They have suckers on them, which made me think of the Sand Witch again and her strange bicycle.

The trip was fun once the ship got under way. Frick and I went to the bow (that's the front, where the half mermaid was) and stood in the salt spray, pretending I was a pirate. When the *Neptune Queen* got out of the harbor she really picked up speed. We had to hold onto the rail sometimes, especially when going crossways through the waves. The boat would smack through them with a loud sound and bounce back just in time for the next one. That part was fun.

It took a couple of hours to get out to where we were supposed to fish, way out of sight of land. After the first hour, it was boring. Waves don't come in many varieties. We explored the ship, which didn't take long, and that's when we ran into Captain Bub.

He grinned at us over a bunch of complicated instruments on the bridge (that's where they drive the boat; it's right on the front, on the second story). He *really* looked like a pirate with an earring and black curly beard and everything.

"Yer kids best keep away from the rail," he snorted. "Ol' Long Ned the man-eatin' shark has sharp eyes for human flesh. That's how I came to lose my trigger finger, so." He held up his hand. It was incomplete.

Frick gulped and backed away from the bucking rail. Of course I didn't believe Captain Bub's yarn, but I backed away too so I wouldn't make Frick look too much like a fraidy-cat. Besides, who knows how high Long Ned *can* jump? Captain Bub just grinned wider.

After a while the boat slowed down and we started circling. Captain Bub used a kind of TV screen that let him see where more fish were. Finally we found the right spot and the engines sputtered off. Frick and I found Dad just in time to help him bait up.

"Just think," Dad said, "below us there are amberjacks and red snappers, and maybe even pompanos looking for food. Let's feed 'em."

Frick and I looked over the side. The water was clear pretty far down, until it got purple from distance. I could tell by the look on Frick's face he was wondering what else was down there, lurking and hungry. So did I.

The rods were heavy, with big motorized reels, but we finally managed to bait up and squeeze between Dad and some fat guy wearing a purple T-shirt with a movie star on it. Everybody was laughing real loud and jostling. I guess they were glad the ride was over, but it seemed to me the boat was rocking more now that we were just floating. It kind of made me queasy.

There wasn't much to do. At least when you fish in a lake or pond you can watch the cork for telltale wiggles. Out on the ocean you have to wait until something jerks your line. The fat guy next to us discovered that crabs can eat the squid arms off your hook without jerking the line at all. And he didn't use phony words like Dad when he was mad.

"Gotta bite!" Dad hissed. He punched the button that hauls the line up, and after a few minutes he pulled up a dripping, rotten old crab trap. Seaweed and barnacles were all over it.

"Furdle," he cursed politely, then brightened. "Hey, there's a crab inside. Oh boy, deviled crab for supper!"

The crab had other ideas. When Dad reached for it, it grabbed his finger with both claws. Dad forgot all his polite curses and used the real ones until the crab let go and splashed over the side.

Frick laughed so hard he almost fell in the bait bucket.

But I didn't feel much like laughing. I didn't feel so good at all. The constant rocking of the boat and all the terrible smells were making my stomach woozy. But I didn't want Dad to make any "little girl" comments, so I just sucked in a long breath and tried to ignore my body.

That was before the fat guy got sick. He made a bizarre noise as if he was calling a pig, lurched a little, and threw up right over the side. It must be awful to be a fish. Anyway, somebody took him to lie down, but that didn't help my stomach. Neither did watching two more people on our side of the boat do the same thing. Soon we were the only ones at the rail.

The rocking got worse. Frick seemed to be immune. He just watched his line where it disappeared in the depths and seemed to keep his footing nicely. Dad couldn't. He was stumbling all over the place. Suddenly Frick noticed how alone we were.

"Hey, what's going on, Dad?" he said. He looked at Dad and laughed. "Wow, I didn't know you could turn green like that—how do you do it?"

Dad's face looked like a breath mint "'Scuse me, kids, but I think I'll rest for a while," he said through clenched teeth and stumbled off.

"What's wrong with everybody?" Frick said as the boat dipped again.

"Urrp . . . froomf," was all I could manage before I lurched after Dad. I had tried to say "seasick."

I don't know if you've ever been seasick. I don't think I can describe it, but it's sort of as if all the flu germs in your town opened an amusement park in your body. Also, your gyros go out and everything spins.

Everyone was moaning in the bunk room, which was right in the front part of the boat so you could feel the waves smacking against the wall. Dad was moaning too. I found an empty bunk right over Dad and slithered in.

The next few hours were awful. The bunk room was dark and cramped. Every time the boat hit a wave, it flew up into the air and then plunged with a terrible noise into the next one. When it hit, there was a chorus of moans from the sick. It sounded like a wolf convention.

"Har! You lubbers are missin' a great show topside," said Captain Bub from the hatch. "We've hit a shoal o' pompano an' there's a wee lad up here reelin' 'em in!"

That had to be Frick. Dad howled and tried to get one leg out of bed. He ended up with his face on the floor; he wasn't going to catch anything this time out.

"Please!" someone groaned to Captain Bub, "I'll give you twenty dollars to take us back!"

Captain Bub laughed "Har! Har! When the *Neptune Queen* sails fer fish, neither squalls nor blasts nor mud-footed lubbers'll turn her back til' the run is done!"

Someone shouted from above and the captain turned. "Hold 'er, lad. Brace yer foot against the rail. I'm comin'!"

After that Captain Bub stuck his head down every few minutes with the Frick Report. "Har! Five pompanos and two rainbow dorados, the count is now!"

"He's catching the whole ocean," Dad whimpered.

Ten minutes later it was, "Ho, lubbers! Th' lad's just landed one o' the prettiest red snappers I've ever seen!"

I think someone threw a shoe at the captain that time.

So it went. I drifted in and out of dreams as the boat pitched. Mostly, they had the Sand Witch in them. I kept remembering that thing Frick found and wondering if it was magic after all. I sure felt cursed. I dozed for a while and when I woke up the boat wasn't rocking the way it had been, but everyone was still sick. I rolled over in time to see Frick coming down the ladder. His eyes were big.

"You aren't going to believe this," he whispered.

"You caught a whale," I moaned.

He looked at me strangely. "No. No, but I did see one.

And guess who was riding its back?" He waited, but all I could do was sigh.

"The Sand Witch," he answered himself with awe in his voice. "Captain Bub had gone for another bucket of squid, and I decided to try a little magic while he was gone. I put the magic medal on instead of a hook, Jenny. But nothing took it, and I was pulling it up when this great big whale came right up to the boat. It had warts all over its chin and it breathed all over me. And . . . and she was riding it. She just smiled when she saw me, then they went back down."

"You're sicker than I am, Frick," I mumbled. "Hallucinations."

"It's true!"

Then Dad woke up. "Frick. Son, is that you? Oh, thank God. Haven't you caught enough fish? Can we please go home?"

"Oh, sure," Frick said. "My arms are tired anyway, and I don't think we could eat any more fish."

"Wonderful," Dad gushed. He sounded like a man in the desert who's just struck water.

"But did you hear what I said, Dad?" Frick added. "I saw a witch riding a whale."

One of Dad's bloodshot eyes peeled open. "Snerk!" was all he said.

Frick got Captain Bub to turn the *Neptune Queen* around, but no one felt any better till she was tied up at a calm dock. It turned out that Frick had caught thirty fish! When the men saw their wives waving from the parking lot, they panicked and started buying fish from him. Frick made nearly a hundred dollars, and we still had a beautiful dorado to take home. It was bigger than Frick. Then Dad gave us both five dollars if we wouldn't tell Mom what had happened. Frick felt so rich he told Dad he could claim the fish if he wanted.

The five dollars didn't make me feel any better until I

got concrete underneath my feet. Even the car felt like it was rocking.

Dad's fish tasted great for supper. But I think it tasted more like crow to him. Mom kept telling him what a great fisherman he was, and he kept trying to be humble.

Frick just stared at his piece of fish vacantly and fingered something in his pocket.

4: A Rhino in Overalls

WE spent the next morning swimming. It was wonderful, just me and Frick and the ocean. There were a lot of waves, and I rode them in my inflatable rubber boat. Sometimes waves would toss the boat right over and I would get water up my nose. But sometimes, if the wave was just right, it would push me all the way to the beach on its crest, just like surfing. Funny, I never even got queasy in my little boat no matter how big the waves were.

I don't think I got out of the water all day. But I kept missing Frick. He would be on top of a dune looking at the new old house. Or, as he put it now, "the witch's house." I could tell he wanted to go exploring there. But I would always call him back. He finally settled on the beach and built a castle.

I wasn't interested in castles right then. I rode the waves. When Dad finally came to get us I was so used to being bounced around, I could hardly walk on the sand. We found the castle, but no Frick. I suddenly got worried, but Dad spotted him a little way down the beach. He was at the inlet where the sea goes in and out of the salt pond. It isn't very wide—just a stream, really.

I started to yell at him, but he turned to us and held out something black.

"It's a shell," he said. "But how could it get burnt underwater?"

Dad looked at the blackened shell warily.

"It must be from the fire she puts under her cauldron," Frick mumbled.

Dad's mouth pursed up, the way adults do when they're disgusted. I guess he was still sore about Frick's fishing luck and his whale story.

"This shell has just been to a clam bake," Dad grumped. "That's all."

"But don't you see," Frick protested, "her ceremonies . . ."

One murderous look from Dad shut us both up until we got back to the cottage. I don't think having more of Frick's fish for supper improved Dad's mood at all.

After supper, though, Dad's disposition brightened. He had us help him move the telescope down to the beach where it would be away from streetlights. "Light pollution" Dad calls it. Dad really enjoys his telescope, as I mentioned. He likes Frick and me to look through it at things he's found. And even though we usually aren't impressed, we oooh and aaah so Dad will be happy.

We moved the telescope just before sunset so it would have time to adjust to the air temperature. Frick and I looked at shells and chased crabs while Dad looked for stars with his binoculars. I watched a sand flea digging his house and got really fascinated. I guess it helps when you're digging to have all those arms. Every time it would go down its hole for another load, I blocked the sand flea's door with sand. It didn't act mad, though. I guess sand fleas are philosophical.

I hadn't even noticed that Frick was looking through the telescope. "Hey," he said. "She . . . she's got a rhino!"

He had the telescope pointed toward "the witch's house," naturally, and I could see the old lady on a distant dune with her dog.

"What are you whooping about?" Dad said, inspecting Frick's use of the telescope.

"A rhino!" Frick insisted, even though I tried to put my hand over his mouth. "The Sand Witch has a little one. You know, they have one horn and little eyes and they live in Africa."

Dad shook his head. "The Sand Witch? Where?" He pointed his binoculars where Frick showed him. "Oh yeah, the little old lady. There's nothing unusual . . ." He paused, and for a minute I thought Frick might not be totally crazy. I strained to make out what was walking beside her. Then Dad said, "That's the ugliest dog I've ever seen."

He had real amazement in his voice, but I could tell Frick was disappointed. It was Alice's Law again. He and Dad were seeing the same thing but interpreting it differently.

It was dark enough now for Dad to be able to locate constellations. He spent a lot of time with star charts and the flashlight before he found the one he was looking for. While he lined up the telescope on it, I tried to get Frick to talk. He wouldn't. He was upset.

Dad found the Owl Nebula, finally. He was really excited, but it was only this real hazy place between some stars. You're supposed to be able to see a face in it, but I couldn't. I oohed anyway. Dad located some galaxies in that constellation which were a little brighter and made notes in his log.

"Now let's see, Virgo should be over there," he mumbled, and wandered over a dune with his binoculars, searching.

Frick lunged for the telescope and pointed it at the salt pond. "I thought he'd *never* go away," he said. "She's got her drapes open."

"Come on, Frick," I said. "There's no witch. Anyway, even if she *is* a witch, she doesn't ride whales and there is no rhinoceros."

'Oh, yes there is," he said as he squinted in the eyepiece. "And he's wearing overalls!"

That was it. I pushed him out of the way and had just focused on the window when Dad came back. He doesn't like us playing with the telescope. He yelled at me.

"It's not a toy," he grumbled.

Boy, and *I* wasn't even the one who had been playing with it. I burnt a look at Frick, but he didn't seem to care. He really looked like he had seen something weird.

Dad found lots more boring galaxies in Virgo. We tried to appreciate them all, faint as they were. But I would have traded every one of them for a rhino in overalls. Finally Dad took his binoculars and went looking for another constellation.

Frick got to the telescope first. I was lookout. He moved the tube around, then stood very still.

"What's the rhinoceros doing now?" I whispered.

"Playing cards," he answered, "with a walrus."

I would have laughed, but by now I knew Frick was either seriously crazy or else Alice's Law was working on me, too. I elbowed him aside and squinted through the eyepiece.

"*Walrus,* eh?" Dad growled.

I looked up and grinned. He was mad now. There was nothing to do but throw ourselves on his mercy.

"HOW MANY TIMES have I told you kids this scope is for looking at the stars! Not in someone's window."

"But, Dad," Frick whined, "it's the witch's house, and the rhino is playing cards with a walrus!"

Dad's look got icy. "Walruses live in the Arctic. It's too hot for them here. AND THEY DO *NOT* PLAY CARDS!"

"This one does," Frick said in a tiny voice. He was looking at the ground. "The witch must have enchanted him."

"That's it," Dad sputtered. "That's it! I'm tired of all this talk about witches and magic and . . . and rhinoceroses!

Give me that scope! We'll see about this." He bent over the telescope, squinting into the eyepiece. "Ha! Just as I thought. No walrus. No rhinoceros. Just a nice old lady on her front porch . . . looking at me."

Dad unsquinted. He looked up and waved sheepishly in the direction of the new old house. He was right; there she was watching the three of us. She waved back.

"Great," he moaned. "Now she thinks she's living next door to a family of Peeping Toms. Well, it's about time you kids cleared all this up. Come on, both of you. I want you to apologize to her for being so nosy."

Up the dunes he marched us. I felt like a condemned prisoner. I hate it when Dad makes us apologize to people. Frick begged and pleaded and warned that we all might be turned into starfish or something when the witch answered the door. I thought about protesting, but Dad doesn't like protesting very much.

There was a long rickety dock out to her house. It swayed on pilings and made lots of noise. I noticed there was an ornate old mailbox, and a name on it: Alie N. All very proper, and un-witchlike. The house looked huge and dark with the full moon rising behind it. The Sand Witch stood waiting for us.

"Hello," she said. She was smiling that smile of hers.

While Dad stumbled through a terrible explanation. I think he was more embarrassed than we were all of a sudden, Frick leaned and stretched, trying to look around her into the house.

Then she laughed. I had never heard anything like that. It wasn't a cackle. It was big and happy. "A walrus? Playing cards with what? Of course, come in and see for yourselves. Delighted."

She opened the door wider. There was no walrus. Just nice old furniture, an aquarium, and a tiny kitchen with a big refrigerator. A dog with a big gray butt was lying in front of the empty hearth.

"Say you're sorry, kids," Dad growled.

We apologized for looking at her with the telescope, Frick with very tight lips. She smiled real big when we were through.

"I'm sorry, too," she said. "I wish I could have shown you a walrus or some magic. But I do have some cookies. Would you like to come in?"

Dad declined. He must have apologized three or four more times. Then we went back to the telescope, Dad still fuming.

"Boy, am I mortified," he said. "I hope you two have learned your lesson about letting your imaginations run loose. Now, I don't want to hear any more talk about witches and walruses, understood?"

He went back to looking for galaxy 4303. To tell the truth, I was glad it was over, too and there was no magic. I hoped maybe we could get down to enjoying our vacation now.

Frick had other plans.

5: Witches and Walruses

"ABSOLUTELY not," I whispered. "I am not sneaking over there in the dead of night. Especially after what Dad said."

It was dark in our bedroom, but I could see Frick's face by moonlight. It was very determined. "Forget about Dad," he said. "Didn't you see—the tide was going out. By now the salt pond will be dry. We can sneak right up to her windows."

"I don't like sneaking," I said. "And I don't like getting caught worse."

"We won't get caught. Listen."

Either Dad was snoring or an alligator was loose in our parents' bedroom again. I still refused. I was tired. Besides, the moon was full, and it wasn't really Dad I was worried about catching us.

Frick frowned. "All right. Who needs you? I'll go by myself."

I could see I was either going to have to tie him up to keep him there or go with him to keep him from getting turned into a starfish or at least caught snooping by the neighbors. I decided to go.

It was late, maybe midnight. The moon was floating right over the funny old house on the salt pond. But there was no water in the pond to reflect the light. Just puddles and lots of shiny shells. A light was on in the house. When the wind blew right, you could hear Wanda singing that song of hers.

30

I got a funny quiver in my spine as we stood on the last dune. Maybe it would be safer to tie Frick up overnight. But it was too late; he was already tiptoeing through the mud. By the time I caught up we were almost at the house.

"It's better to go this way anyway," Frick whispered. "The pier's too noisy."

"Sssh," I said, gulping. All I could think of was how obvious we looked in the moonlight.

Then the house was looming right over us. I stood on tiptoe and tried looking in the lighted window, but it was way too high. I looked down and noticed Frick squatting underneath the house beside a piling.

"Look, Jenny," he said. "All the shells down here are black."

They were, too. Everything under the house was covered with soot and charred. Frick snapped off a piece of mud and handed it to me. It was all hard and smooth on one side like glass.

"Melted?" I wondered. I had heard about sand around atomic bomb sites being melted into glass.

Frick gulped loudly. "M-maybe it wasn't such a good idea to come here." He glanced around at the shadows.

"Oh, no," I said. "You're not going to chicken out now. Not just when I'm starting to get interested. Whatever this stuff is, it didn't come from a witch's cauldron. Come on. Boost me up so I can look in the window."

Frick started whining about being littler than me, but I reminded him he had already seen the walrus. It was about time I saw some of this witch stuff. He had got me out in the middle of a muddy pond at midnight to see a witch, and I was going to see one!

"Higher," I said.

Frick grumbled and raised up some, wobbling. It felt good to finally have him doing something for me. After all . . .

There was a rhinoceros, all right.

He was in the kitchen making a ham sandwich, right under the light. He was wearing overalls, and he had a ring through his horn. I almost fell off Frick. I grabbed the ropes strung between pilings and leaned right up close to the window. The rhino said something. I swear.

It sounded like, "Oh, stop *kvetching*. It's not *that* hot."

He was talking to the walrus. At first I had thought the walrus was a sofa or something else big, but he moved when the rhino spoke to him. He was looking in the witch's aquarium and fanning himself with one of those Japanese paper fans. The green light from the aquarium reflected off his tusks. I didn't see the witch anywhere. "What's happening? Frick wiggled. "See the walrus?"

I kicked him in the nose, gently. I didn't want anything to interrupt the show.

The walrus huffed. He moved from side to side impatiently. "That's easy for you to say," he said to the rhino, "you're hot-blooded. My blood is boiling." He had a nasal tone. He sighed. "Why doesn't Stan come? Something must be wrong... you don't suppose Edgar has done something foolish?"

"Naah," the rhino said as he tried to get the last bit of mayonnaise out of the jar. "Stop worrying; you won't be here much longer. We'll locate Edgar, you'll talk him into returning, and you can get back home to the ice."

By now my nose was almost touching the glass. This was fascinating. I forgot I was peeking in a window at midnight. It was like a rerun of *The Twilight Zone*. Suddenly the walrus wheezed, "I can't stand it! I need cool air!"

I didn't know walruses could move that quick. Before I could budge he had flopped over to the window and slid it up. He stuck his head out and inhaled so hard he sucked

my face into his nose. It was wet, and it smelled like an anchovy pizza.

"Blecchh!" I pulled back.

I looked at him and blinked. He blinked back. His eyes got wider and wider. I smiled and said hello. I think that's what panicked him.

First, he howled. It sounded like a siren in a barrel. Then Frick gave way, freaked by the noise, and I dangled from the ropes. All I could see through the window was the rhino's surprised face as the walrus ran into him. BLAM! they hit, and ham sandwich flew all over the kitchen.

That was the last thing I saw before I fell on top of Frick. What with the mud and the walrus's howl still echoing across the pond, we managed to knock each other down twice before the light hit us. It shone over the rope railing of the house, dazzling us.

"Why, hello," said a calm voice. "You must have decided on some cookies after all. How friendly of you."

I swallowed heavily. She had us now. I thought about making a run for it, but she was so quiet and unexcited there didn't seem much point in it. She acted like nothing at all was wrong. I took the chance. By now, I really did want to find out what was going on.

So, with Frick squeezing my hand purple, we went inside. No walrus. No rhino. Just Wanda, beaming, and lots of neat old furniture. But there was a card table with two chairs set up, and a deck of tarot cards spread out on it.

"Welcome to my . . . home," she said.

Frick let go of my hand and stepped forward. He was real pale, but you had to admire his spunk. "Look," he said. "We know you're a witch. We saw those animals in here, and we heard you fly over our house."

She looked from Frick to me with those pale, unblinking eyes. "You too?"

I nodded. "I was the one who scared your walrus."

Her shoulders shook when she laughed, and her skin crinkled up around her eyes.

"And you dropped a magic medal down our chimney," Frick added. He fished the thing out of his pocket with shaky hands and held it out. "Did you hex us?"

I waited for her to explode. But she grinned even wider. She looked delighted that we had discovered she was a witch.

"You found it!" she squeaked, and gratefully took the metal thing from Frick. "I couldn't imagine where I lost it. This is indeed a load off my mind. Thank you."

I looked at Frick. I could tell his theories about her were coming undone.

"Cookies, please?" she said. She held out a giant bowl loaded with big animal-shaped cookies.

Frick and I looked at each other. Were witches supposed to behave like this? We each took a cookie and sat down on the plush velveteen sofa. They tasted great. Wanda hooked the metal thing on a prong on her belt, then sat across from us. She munched on a frosted elephant, staring dreamily into space.

"You're absolutely right," she said to no one in particular. "I am a witch. It's so nice of you to notice. People seem very indifferent to us nowadays. If they see anything unusual, they pretend not to notice. I suppose they've been ruined by so many phoney witches running around having seances. And TV, of course. Color TV is magic enough for some people."

Frick's mouth dropped open and a piece of cookie fell out. Even he never thought he was really right about her. "You mean you really *are* a witch? But you're so nice! And witches aren't supposed to admit they are, are they?" He looked at me. I shrugged. He continued, "You sure didn't give Dad the idea you were a witch."

She shrugged. "He didn't really want to know. I certainly didn't deny it to him."

"But where's your cauldron and your broomstick?"

She sighed. "Those were in the good old days, when we were *really* under cover."

At that point something thumped in the kitchen. I jumped. But it was only the rhino peering over a cupboard (you know something's wrong when a rhinoceros in overalls seems normal). I realized he had been the gray "dog" I had seen when Dad had barged us in before.

"Oh. Kids, meet Bob," Wanda said.

Bob grumbled a greeting. He had mayonnaise on his horn. His name was written over his chest pocket in red thread, like on a mechanic's overalls. He really wasn't as big as a regular rhino, more like the size of a St. Bernard.

"Where's Dan?" Wanda asked him.

"Where else?" Bob said in a gravelly voice and opened the refrigerator. Snow fluttered out. "Come on out, fatso," Bob said, "and help me get the sandwich off the wall."

A whiskered nose emerged. "But it's nice in here. Are the people gone?"

"Hello," I said.

The walrus flinched, but he finally came out of the refrigerator. Bob resumed his sandwich making, grumbling. Dan, the walrus, acted embarrassed and pretended not to notice us.

I wasn't embarrassed, just surprised that I was getting used to talking to rhinoceroses. I had another cookie, this one shaped like an octopus. Frick had started on a lobster.

"But I never read anything about witches and rhinos," Frick said. "It's always supposed to be black cats, or frogs and bats. Is Bob a pet of yours—"

Bob snorted and looked sharply at Frick.

"Or—what do they call them, Jenny?"

"Familiars," I said. (I had to write a report on witches last Halloween.)

"Yeah, a familiar?"

"Yes, they used to call them that." Wanda smiled. "It's nice to hear the old words again. Makes me long for my broomstick. But no, Bob and Dan aren't familiars. They're more like colleagues, really. You see, we're looking for someone who shouldn't be here. His name is Edgar. Bob is great at tracking and digging through sand with his horn."

Suddenly I remembered those clouds of sand that gave her her name. She had been tracking somebody . . . or something.

"And Dan," she continued, "is here from his home in Alaska to help. He knew Edgar in the old days. We thought maybe he could talk Edgar into coming back, if we had located him tonight."

"I still say Edgar's too stubborn for that," Dan honked. "You know borxnees, once they've got something in their pinchers they never let go."

For some reason, a shiver tickled my neck. I was about to ask what a borxnee was, when the alarm went off. Frick and I collided in midair trying to get away. It was only an oven timer, but it was loud, and being around a real witch sort of makes you nervous.

"Well, I guess Stan can't make it tonight," Wanda said, getting up from her seat. "He said tonight or tomorrow night and by this time, so you might as well go home, Dan."

The walrus *smiled*. More tusk showed, and the blubber bunched up around his eyes "Home. Cool white ice. Hoooo!"

"Sorry you had to come for nothing," Wanda soothed, and opened the refrigerator door as if she was showing him out. "We'll call you tomorrow if we locate Edgar."

Snow flurried out of the fridge again. A gust of icy air

whipped out with it. Dan clapped his flippers with joy and flopped right into the refrigerator. I leaned around the door. There were no trays inside with leftovers on them or compartments. There was no inside. Just a lot of white going off to the horizon and the shape of Dan disappearing into the snow. I blinked.

Frick made very puzzled whining noises and Wanda turned to us. She looked very surprised like she didn't know humans could make noises like that. Then she saw my expression. "Oh, of course. You're wondering where Dan went. This is his doorway home." She closed the door, adjusted a dial on a weird-looking control panel on the side, and opened it again. Now it was full of metal trays and food. Bob put the mayonnaise in it.

"I guess it's time for us to go," I said reluctantly.

"Oh, but won't you come up with us?" Wanda said to Frick and me. "There's room. You could help me search. And you would be such nice company."

Bob snorted at that.

"Up?" Frick squeaked. I think he was still thinking of broomsticks. The shock of all his suspicions turning real was getting to him.

"Yeah," I jumped in quickly. "We'll go with you and look for Edgar. Sure."

She beamed. Bob frowned and scratched his horn. Rhinos are even uglier when they frown. Then he and Wanda busied themselves with some crates in a corner, banging around.

Frick pulled frantically at my sleeve. "But, Jenny! You didn't even want to come here tonight. Let's go home. I feel weird."

I shushed him. "Look, I came, didn't I? Now let's clear up these mysteries while we have the chance. Don't worry, she's not going to turn us into anything. I don't think she's that kind of witch. I sort of like her, to tell the truth."

6: Stories in the Stars

THERE we were, preparing to go into the sky with a witch and a pygmy rhinoceros to look for someone, or something, named Edgar. I don't know if it was my being up so late or the shock of it all, but I felt sort of woozy. Frick looked dazed. Alice's Law was working on him: everything looked normal, the way it does to grown-ups, but it wasn't. But I could tell behind his glazed eyes that computer brain of his was busy.

Wanda and Bob had unpacked a bunch of equipment. We followed them into a little room that turned out to be the bathroom, where they dropped all the tools. Bob wiggled out of his overalls. I didn't know whether to be embarrassed or not. Wanda tied a rope from a big rubber plunger to the scruffy end of Bob's tail. Then she dipped the plunger in water and stuck it to the back rim of the tub. It made a loud popping noise.

"Did you see under it?" Frick whispered. "It had lots of small cups under it instead of one big one. Like her bicycle tires."

Bob got in the bathtub. He stretched his arms and did breathing exercises that made his cheeks puff out. He was very businesslike. It reminded me of yoga, which I've seen Mom do. When he was through, he clicked a chain leash from his nose ring to the shower pipe. It didn't come out of the wall, it was just a naked pipe that went up beside the tub.

"Ready for lift-off, Ranger Wanda," he said. He was suddenly so official!

"Roger, Bob," she said, smiling.

She winked at us. Then she unscrewed the shower pipe from its fitting with a huge wrench. The part that went into the wall was shaped sort of like an *S,* and she grabbed the end and twisted. Slowly, it turned.

I heard a groan overhead and Frick punched me. The roof was slowly sliding over on metal grooves. Stars showed.

"She's cranking it open," Frick whispered.

I think I felt weirder right then than I ever had in my life. I didn't have any idea what was going on. Unless the bathtub was going to be launched into space with Bob as pilot. Maybe the chain and rope were like a seat belt. Maybe I was going crazy.

I was about to ask, when Wanda squeaked the shower head around backwards and said, "Engage."

Bob shut his eyes and started inhaling. His cheeks got puffier and puffier. As a matter of fact, all of him was getting puffier. His face was ballooning, his body was ballooning. He was a pasty color, and getting bigger all the time. I felt my hair rising. Frick whimpered and stumbled for the door. I grabbed him.

"It's quite all right." Wanda smiled. "He's a puffernoceros."

I don't know why that should calm anyone. Bob was bigger than the bathtub now, and he was floating at the ends of his tethers. It was like he was a balloon. He filled the hole where the roof had been. The tub lifted one porcelain foot off the floor, then another.

Wanda stepped into the tub and the feet banged back down. "Come on, we're about to lift off."

I pulled Frick into the tub with me and we huddled at the back. I looked up. No stars, just puffernoceros. Then I felt a funny jar. The room wobbled; everything started moving down past us. No, we were floating! The whole tub, us inside, was being lifted by Bob!

"We have lift-off," Wanda announced.

Up, up, out of the bathroom entirely. The wind tickled us. We were above Wanda's house.

"Engage hydropropulsion," Wanda said, and turned the shower on. Water spewed out, the tub kicked forward.

"Hey, we're moving," Frick said.

"Newton's Third Law." She grinned. "The shower pushes us."

Nobody asked her where the water came from. I guessed it was either magic or the pipes condensed it out of the air. We passed over her house, and Wanda headed us out toward the beach. The other faucet turned the shower left or right. There were some dunes below, and then our cottage, dead ahead. The shower pattered water across the sea oats. The sound reminded me of something familiar, but foggy, like a dream. I looked at Frick.

A little light went on in his brain. "I know how you lost that magic medal down our chimney!" he announced to Wanda. She smiled back. "You took this same trip Friday night, didn't you?"

She nodded. "Just after we arrived."

I looked at him, puzzled. He pointed ahead of us. It was the eave of our cottage, right over our bedroom. "You were too low then, and hit the edge of the roof."

Frick's discovery delighted her. "Yes. Exactly right. I carried far too much equipment with me the first time. Made things too heavy."

As it was, we cleared the eave by only about six inches. It made me hold my breath.

"You musta been leaning over the edge of the tub like this," he said, and acted it out. "And the weathervane hooked the metal thing off your belt . . ." He flicked the

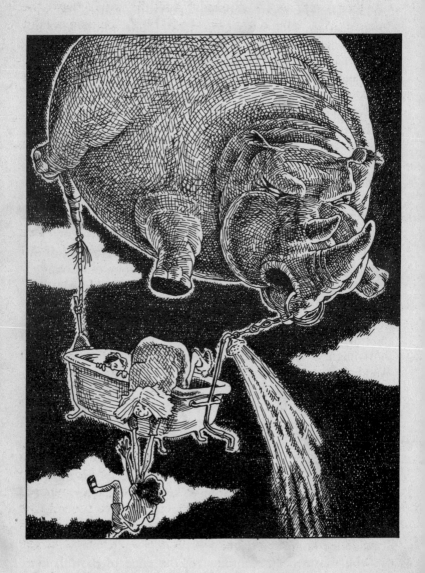

weather vane as he passed. "And the wind blew the weather vane around until the medal hit the chimney and it toppled in."

Mystery number one bit the dust.

Wanda laughed and applauded. Frick grinned and sat back down, and when he did, the tub wobbled in the other direction. I fell out.

Everything spun, and I don't care what anybody says, you can't scream when you're falling. I tried. But then I realized I was being hauled back into the tub. Wanda, with her long spindly arms, had caught me. My heart played march music anyway.

But we were rising faster all the time. I turned to see the cottage dwindling. It looked like a Monopoly token. After I recovered from almost falling down the chimney, I asked her about Bob.

"Where he comes from all rhinos can become airborne," she answered. "You see, he's not transplanted." That smile again.

I didn't see, but before I could ask more, she began looking over the side and said, "I hope we have more luck than Bob and I had—what did you call it—Friday night. Actually, we haven't seen any sign of Edgar at all."

"Uh, what does Edgar look like, exactly," I asked.

"Oh, he's big, about the size of a car. You would recognize him as a crab. Just look for a big crab."

I swallowed. Great. There was a giant crab loose on Summer Island. Just like in *Attack of the Crab Monsters* on TV. I looked over the side. We were a couple of hundred feet up, following the coast north. I could see several cars and vans parked on the beach, but no giant crabs. Wanda used a rusty old spyglass and hummed to herself as she searched.

Frick wasn't searching. He had that distant look in his

eyes. I sure hoped he could figure out what was going on. I couldn't.

Then, almost as if he knew what I was thinking, he pulled me close to him and whispered, "I know what's going on, Jenny. Wanda's a witch all right, but that's just her cover. That's to scare people away. She's really an alien."

"I don't understand," I said. "Where's her spaceship if she's an alien?"

"I dunno," he replied, as though that was just a minor detail. "But she said she arrived Friday night. Remember the long meteor, the one from Hydra?"

That clicked. Everything began making a lot more sense.

"Then Edgar..." I began.

Frick nodded. "He's alien, too. He escaped from wherever she's from—the constellation Hydra, I guess. It's her job to hunt him down and bring him back with her. The puffernoceros is from there, too."

Something was bothering me. "What about Dan?" I said. "The walrus? His home was Alaska. That isn't alien."

Frick shrugged. That didn't seem to bother him at all. He would wait until he had more evidence on that, the precocious little punk.

I began to feel less mystified, anyway. Maybe he was right about the aliens.

After that we helped her search for Edgar, but we must have traveled for over an hour and didn't see anything like a giant crab. We passed a city and then Wanda turned the shower around when we started passing a lot of swamps and marshes. ("Edgar would hate that," she said.) Nobody ever noticed us floating over, but we sure surprised some gulls.

The moon had risen higher. It was real big up there, and full. I felt I could almost reach out and touch it. I stopped looking for Edgar, since we were heading back where we had already searched. I looked at the moon. Dad had taught us most of the craters names.

"Wow. Tycho looks so huge," I commented.

Wanda glanced around. "Tycho? Who's that?"

Frick and I laughed. "It's not a person," I said. "It's a crater on the moon, the big one with all the rays."

She still looked puzzled.

"You know—one of the craters, the big holes where meteorites hit the moon a long time ago."

She understood. Then she turned her face up to the moon and laughed real long and hard. I thought she was crazy. How do you tell if an alien is crazy?

"Oh, yes," she finally chuckled, wiping away a tear. "I forgot how many stories there are about your moon. Long ago, they thought a dragon ate the moon every month. And once when I was stationed here, it was thought that if you let moonlight fall on your face while you slept, it would melt your brain."

Frick laughed at that.

"But what does that have to do with craters?" I said. I didn't like being laughed at without knowing why.

"You said they were made by falling rocks." Wanda smiled.

"Well? They *were* made by falling rocks. Big rocks. Like a storm of meteorites."

"Then why doesn't the earth have as many?" she said, then laughed again. "Actually, there are some . . . craters like that on the moon. But most were made by bahoogies."

It got real quiet in the tub.

"You see, once your moon was smooth all over. But then it was in another solar system, a neighbor to yours. In that solar system lived a family of bahoogies. If you imagine an octopus so big that it could wrap its legs around the earth and be able to touch tips, that's what a bahoogie is like.

They have very tough skin and make their own air inside them, so they can live in space.

"The only thing is, space is *boring*. So bahoogies invented lots of games they could play. There was fawinki, like marbles only played with asteroids. And they had a game called hooploop that was like ringtoss with planets. You have a planet in this system that they played hooploop with."

"Saturn?" Frick interrupted.

"That's the one. Anyway, their favorite game was suckerball. It was sort of like basketball. A small planet was used as the ball. One team tried to score a goal by throwing the planet into the sun, and the other team had to stop them. The sun was the goal; one day your moon was picked to play with. It was a long game, and lots of bahoogies played. They had all sizes of suckers, and back then your moon was sort of sticky and muddy. So it got sucker marks of all different sizes all over it. Finally, someone tried to make a goal with it, but it *just* missed the sun. It kept on going, and finally was trapped by earth's magnetic field. It's been here ever since, with all those sucker marks all over it."

"That's not scientific, though!" I objected.

"But it's true," she said. "Things are seldom what they seem. It depends on who's looking at them." That made me think of Alice. "But even your people remember suckerball. There's an old game that comes from the time of the bahoogies. You try to kick a sphere into a net that represents the sun's gravity. It's played with a ball covered with white and black sucker marks."

"You mean soccer?" I said.

She smiled. "No, sucker."

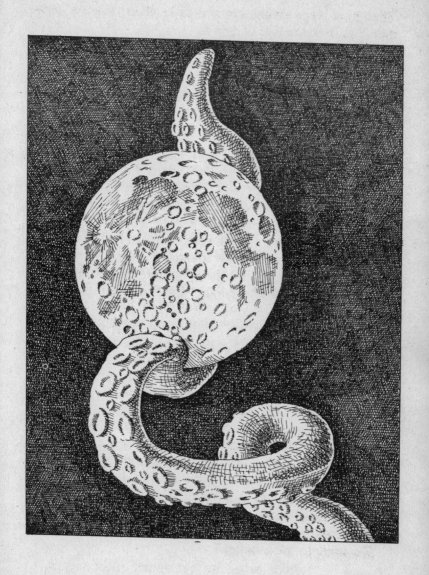

7: Mission from Hecate

THERE wasn't any getting around it. There was a witch next door. Only she was really an alien pretending to be a witch so no one would notice how weird she was. And she had a pygmy rhinoceros who could become a balloon so that they could search for a giant crab. Suddenly, my vacation had gotten complicated.

After sleeping until noon the next day, we had to go with Mom and Dad to visit some friends of theirs. Frick pestered me with questions all the way there. Was it all real? How did Wanda get here? Why did Edgar escape? Who was Stan?

I had to threaten to punch him to get him to shut up. After all, he's supposed to be the precocious one. I had my own questions. I didn't buy any of that garbage about bahoogies making the craters on the moon. But then, I had seen Bob with my own eyes, and the refrigerator to Alaska was real, too. Maybe the bahoogies were like a fairy tale where she came from.

But it was no use. My own questions bothered me as much as Frick's did. And there was only one person who could answer them all. As much as I didn't want to, I knew we'd be visiting Wanda again.

The visit with Mom and Dad's friends was boring. They had a kid, but he was a spoiled brat. It was awful pretending to enjoy playing with him.

It was nearly dark when we got home. After supper, I asked if we could go next door and visit Wanda.

Dad's eyebrows went up. "The witch? Aren't you afraid she'll stew you?"

"Nah," I said. "She's sort of nice when you get to know her. Besides, she tells good stories."

"And makes good cookies," Frick added.

"Well, I'm glad to see you two realize your imaginations ran away with you," Dad said. "You must learn to see things the way they really are. By the way, I want you home before ten. Don't forget we have a rematch with the *Neptune Queen* tomorrow morning."

I made unhappy noises. I didn't want to go to sea again. I had thrown up enough for one vacation. I think Dad wanted to prove to us that he could catch as many fish as Frick.

We ran to Wanda's house, bouncing along the noisy pier this time. The house wasn't scary like before, even with the full moon behind it. Wanda smiled just as widely. She wore the same dress and slippers.

"Any luck?" Frick asked.

Her smile faded a little as she poured us some tea from a fancy copper kettle. "Ah, no. Not a sign of Edgar. Not a candy wrapper or a Popsicle stick. I went on my bicycle in the opposite direction we traveled last night. I went the longest way. Then, Bob and I checked the dunes again. Edgar burrows, you know."

Bob, who was playing solitaire with the tarot cards, blew his nose sharply. It sounded like he had sand packed in his sinuses. He didn't seem happy.

As a matter of fact, Wanda looked unhappier than ever before, too. Her smile was sort of bent. I took a sip of tea (it tasted like walnuts) and asked, "Exactly who is Edgar, anyway?"

She sighed. "A romantic. A runaway. A truant. He was under my care, but he thinks things where he lives are dull.

No excitement, he says. Would you like to see some home movies of him?"

Frick chirped like a bird. "Yes! Yes! Show us!"

That brought a full smile back to her face. She did something to the handle of the teapot in front of her, twisted it or something. Suddenly, the spout flickered. Light came out of it and made this image right in the middle of the room. It was like a slide, only not flat. You could see all the way around the picture. A red and purple crab was standing in front of the fireplace.

"Edgar," she said fondly.

He was hopping around on the tops of things that looked like mushrooms. Somebody was throwing him something like a pair of bright blue cups tied together. He was catching them. It was a game.

"You can see how playful he is," she said.

The scene changed. Edgar was indoors, eating some kind of stuff that looked like green crystals. He was waving his antennas like I would if I was a happy crab.

"Loves candy," she said. "That's diggyhoo, about the only kind of candy we have at home. There are lots more kinds here."

The scene changed again. Edgar was in some sort of terminal. People who looked sort of like Wanda were walking around him, wearing strange clothes. He was waving. A big train of some kind came into the station behind him. It made a loud noise, and Edgar jumped right into the air.

"He's so nervous." Wanda chucked. "Hates loud noises. But he loves crowds and excitement, parties and festivities. The kind of events you have here on Earth."

Frick gasped. Again, I don't think he really believed his own theory. But there was Wanda, admitting she was an alien.

"But why did Edgar come to Earth?" I asked. "And how did he get here?"

"Edgar used to live here," Wanda replied, "many years ago." When she saw how puzzled Frick and I still were, she added, "Perhaps I had better explain everything."

"Please start at the beginning," I said.

Her eyes got a faraway look, even further away than normal. "In the beginning was a great darkness."

"Not that far back."

"Oh. Of course. Well, I told you that we witches were always misunderstood. That is because we have been visiting Earth for millions of years. We could always do a lot more than you natives because we were so much more advanced. We let you think it was magic. We used to ride small rocket packs that looked like broomsticks to the peasants. And we cooked our own food, the food of Hecate, in big pots. It wasn't anything like Earth food, and got a bad reputation. And our uniforms were black."

"Uniforms?" Frick said.

"Yes. You see, we are really like park rangers. Earth is unique. Most planets have two or three different climates. Earth has hundreds. We have been visiting Earth for millions of years. We have been exploring the rest of the galaxy for a long time, too. It's a big place, you know. So, whenever we found a species that was dying out on its home world, we brought it here. Here, species flourish. Earth is a shelter world for endangered species."

"What are you talking about?" I shouted. I must have sounded hysterical. How could my planet be like a cosmic zoo without us knowing? "What species?"

Bob laughed, kind of a gritty sound. He daubed at his snout with a tissue.

"Rhinoceroses, for one," she said. "They are from Ras Algheti. Remember Dan? Walruses are from Castor IV. We brought small bahoogies here when their race was almost wiped out by cosmic rays. You call them octopuses."

Frick laughed. He seemed to be catching on. "What about platypuses?"

"From Fomalhaut."

"Bats?"

"Karundi X."

My mind was spinning. "Wait a minute! What about Darwin? What about evolution?"

"Oh, most Earth creatures are native," she said. "As I said, Earth has more different environments than anywhere else. But you can tell the extraterrestrials. They appear very unusual alongside Earth animals.

"And we only bring creatures here until we can find a better place for them to live. We locate new home worlds for them. Some stay here only a few hundred years. It didn't take long to find another home planet for the unicorns of Vega. They only stayed two hundred years, in the Middle Ages. The sphinxes were here for thousands of years before we resettled them."

"Oh, I get it." Frick blinked. "When you take a creature away, it becomes a legend. Everybody now just thinks unicorns were a story."

Wanda nodded. "Unless they stay so long here that they leave fossils. You know about dinosaurs? They live happily in their new home on the other side of the galaxy. They're just discovering space travel."

"And you found a new home for Edgar the same way?" Frick asked.

"Yes." Wanda smiled. "Edgar is a borxnee. There haven't been any borxnees on Earth now for quite a while. They're all on Antares XI. All of them except Edgar, at least. He stowed away on a tourist ship a week ago. We know he got off in this vicinity."

"Tourist ship?" I said weakly.

"Oh, yes. Earth is very popular as a tourist spot. People from all over the galaxy come to see this assortment. It's very difficult to get permission to visit, though. Too many earthlings notice."

"UFOs?" I asked.

"I think that's what you call them." She nodded.

I felt strange. Alice's Law was bigger than just the difference between kids and grown-ups. Wanda had a completely different interpretation for my world than I did. And yet I couldn't prove her wrong. I even kind of believed her. All except her explanation for the craters on the moon. I looked at Frick, and you could tell he was swallowing everything. He loved it.

Wanda sighed. "And now I have to take Edgar back. He has to learn to like his new home. But where could he be? Bob hasn't been able to even pick up a trace."

"Hasn't been here," Bob grunted. "Not on the beach."

Wanda threw up her hands. "But he has to be around water. He needs to stay wet."

That's when the aquarium erupted. There was a rumble, then water exploded everywhere and something made this horrible mooing sound. Like a giant bull. I didn't see what it was. I was behind the couch. But I could hear Frick making excited noises.

"Neat!" he squealed. "It's the whale!"

I peeked over the sofa. There was an eye the size of a baseball looking out of the aquarium. And a big warty black hump rose from the top and *breathed*. It freaked me out all over again, making sounds like a vacuum cleaner.

Wanda leaned over it. I tried to warn her back, but she just laughed. "Stan!" she said, "it's good to see you again. We expected you last night."

The warty, lumpy place mooed and gasped.

"You did!" Wanda seemed delighted. "Where was he? What was he doing?"

More mooing and snorting. It sounded like a stampede.

"Very good, Stan!" she said. "I'll notify Dan. We'll meet you tomorrow at the usual place, in the morning."

Stan hooted and then sort of yodeled a growl.

"Same to you." She smiled.

Then the hump sank, along with the eye. The aquarium was murky for a second, then the tropical fish and toy castles reappeared.

"What was *that?*" I said, standing.

"A whale!" Frick grinned. "The one I saw Wanda riding when I went fishing with the magic medal."

"Yes. Quite right," Wanda said. "I had forgotten you saw us. We followed your bait. We were out looking for Edgar. But Stan just told me he's found signs of Edgar!"

My heart was beginning to beat normally again. "Are you telling me that a whole whale fit in that aquarium?"

"Not all of him. Impossible. There's just enough room for his blowhole. The aquarium works just like the refrigerator does. You see, we relocated the whales to earth, too."

I blinked.

"Can we go with you tomorrow and meet Stan?" Frick begged. I tried to kick him.

"Of course you can," Wanda said. "Love to have you. There should be enough room for all of us."

I gulped. I wasn't sure I wanted to go *under* the sea. I liked the beach just fine. Just enough water to get you wet.

"I-I don't think we'd better," I said. "We don't know anything about snorkels or scubas and stuff like that."

Bob and Wanda just laughed. "You don't need to know any of that," she said. "You don't even need a swimsuit. Leave everything to me and you won't even get wet. Just meet me on the beach at nine."

8: To the Bottom in a Bubble

DAD got really mad when we told him we didn't want to go out on the *Neptune Queen* with him. His nose turned purple

"What's a vacation for?" he said. "You don't want to have any fun? Okay, okay. Stay at home! I'll catch all the fish, then."

A bunch of his friends picked him up so Mom could use the car. They looked a lot like the first group of clods we'd gone fishing with. I was glad we weren't going. But I wasn't at all sure I wanted to go to the bottom of the sea, either. I trusted Wanda a lot more now, but even witches can make mistakes. Even nice witches.

"Maybe she's got a submarine hidden wherever she's got her rocket hidden," Frick wondered as we walked to the beach. "Or maybe she's got a magic snorkel so we can breathe underwater."

I was trying to think of a way to stay home without Frick thinking I was scared. But there was Wanda on top of a sand dune, Dan the walrus beside her. She saw us and waved in a very unfamiliar way, with the side of her hand. I guessed it must be a Hecatean greeting.

"*Pogwom weeto*, as we say where I come from. Greetings," she said. "Bob can't follow a scent underwater, so he's staying at home, but Dan here can help us if we see Edgar. They were great friends in the old days."

Dan just turned his nose up and sniffed at a big gray rain cloud that was floating our way.

That gave me an idea. "Uh, maybe we'd better not go out today," I said. "Looks like a thunderstorm."

Wanda just smiled, sort of chuckling to herself. "Oh, that won't bother us at all. Not where we're going."

Lightning cracked on the horizon and Dan flinched. "It may not bother us there, but it sure bothers me here. Let's get on with it." He shuffled nervously from flipper to flipper.

Frick clapped gleefully. He was really wired up for this expedition. Wanda took a purple plastic bottle out of a pocket. There was a little wire loop inside it, like a bubble blower.

"Bunch up together," she said. We did.

She dipped the loop, then began blowing through it. A pinkish bubble fluttered out. But Wanda kept blowing so it never had time to pop out of the loop. It just got bigger and bigger. It had rainbows all over it, like a film. They wavered. Wanda kept blowing steadily. Soon the bubble was as big as a tire, then as big as a car. It just fluttered past all of us until we were on the inside of a big pink dome. Wanda stopped blowing and twisted the loop. The bubble came off. We stood on the sand with a pink wall around us.

"There," she said, satisfied. "A mongoolian-fraztnoy tension sphere. It will repel water and move with our bodies."

The world was tinted pink. There was pink lightning on the horizon. I looked nervously at Wanda. "You mean we are supposed to just walk out into the ocean with this thing around us?"

"Exactly," she replied, quite pleased with the bubble.

"But, the pressure . . ." I said. "And what if a fish swims into it?"

"Oh, fish are afraid of it," she said. "The blatikkid flow, you know."

"Let's go," Frick gurgled.

We began walking toward the surf. I thought about making a run for it, but decided Frick would always think I was a coward if I did. Besides, I told myself, it'll be a great experience. It started raining as we walked into the surf. The drops just seemed to roll off the pink wall of the bubble. And it held back the ocean just like an upside-down fishbowl. It moved with our bodies, keeping us in its middle.

That doesn't mean it wasn't scary. At first it was neat, the way the water just separated and went around us. When we got deeper, it was like that scene in *The Ten Commandments* when the Red Sea parted. I thought for sure the bubble would pop, but it held. The waves splashed right over the top. I kept expecting to feel the waves falling on top of us at any minute, but after a while I got used to walking in the bubble. I noticed something clenched in my hand. It was Frick's hand. I guess he was a little scared, too.

Wanda started humming cheerfully. And Dan seemed more relaxed than before. His eyes didn't look so wide and surprised. Maybe he felt more at home down here.

Everything was green outside the bubble. Nearby was clear green, hazing out to a foggy green far off. Fish swam by just like in an aquarium. When they got close to the pink wall, though, they acted surprised and swam away. Maybe it shocked them or smelled funny or something. Anyway, I started believing again that Wanda knew what she was talking about.

"Now, we just have to walk about a kilometer this way," Wanda said. "Then we turn left by the coral tree. Stan should be waiting."

"Good," Dan snuffed. "Get this over with. It's even hot under all this water. I hope you keep better watch on Edgar after all this."

"This is neat," Frick gasped as a lobster shot by. An

octopus was chasing it. "It's even better than *Wild King-dom.*"

"Yes." Wanda sighed. "The water world is very beautiful. And peaceful. My own Hecate is a world of wide lakes and canals. Our homes are partly in the water."

"Is that why you have webbed fingers?" I asked.

"My, but you are observant." Her eyes twinkled.

After a while the water got a darker green. We were deeper. We passed an old wrecked ship with lots of fish hanging around it. In one place, about a thousand crabs cleared a path for our bubble. Then we came to the coral tree. It was beautiful, like an oak tree made of pink marble. And it had purple fans all over it and lots of fish swimming in its branches. We turned left there.

A shadow passed over us. There were lots of wavery shadows from the waves, so I didn't look up until Frick punched me. Then Wanda's water world didn't seem so peaceful anymore.

"W-Wanda," I gulped, "sh-shark!"

It was just like in the movies, circling us with those mean beady eyes. I felt my heart playing taps.

"Ulp," said Dan, with a kind of blubbery shiver. His eyes got wide again.

The shark was down where we were now. He casually circled the bubble, pretending not to be interested. I knew better.

"Calm, now." Wanda smiled.

She didn't look worried at all. But that didn't make me feel any better. She wasn't carrying any weapon that I could see, and that shark looked big and hungry. Suddenly, he swam right for us. He stopped in front of the bubble. He tried to bite it.

I screamed. Frick whimpered.

Wanda snorted and scrunched up her eyebrows. She looked mad. She took out the bubble blower and blew through it at a place on the bubble. A seam opened up there, a break in the soapy film, only no water came in. The shark came close to watch. I think he was as surprised as we were when Wanda stuck her head out of the bubble. I know he was surprised when she bit his nose because he backed away real fast like someone touching a flame.

Frick clapped and I took a long breath. Wanda pulled her head back in, shook out her hair, and grinned. But the shark was still out there. He was making wider, more respectful circles. Wanda put her hands on her hips and growled. I thought she was about to climb right out of the bubble, but something happened first.

It was a low snorting noise. Then it got louder and louder, and faster and faster. It ended like a siren. Something big was coming. Part of the ocean got dark, and then an eye appeared in the darkness. The shark got real nervous and left.

"Stan!" Wanda shouted. "*Pogwom weeto*, my friend!"

The whale swam closer and growled his greetings. His tail disappeared in the mist. Then there was a lot of discussion with Dan's wheezing snorts mixed in with the whale's groans. I think that was the moment I started believing walruses and whales could really be alien creatures.

After the discussion, we followed Stan. "He's found Edgar's hideout," Wanda said excitedly.

We had to run part of the way, with Stan's tail swishing the bubble back and forth. Finally, we came to a rocky cliff. There was a crack in it. As we walked around the crack, we could see it got wider and wider. Stan honked and trumpeted.

"He says he's seen Edgar go in there," Wanda translated. "Dan, see if he's in. Talk to him. Reason with him."

Dan rolled his eyes and snorted. "Hmmmf! And what if there's a nasty moray eel in there instead? Why do I have to go in alone? Why must I take all the risks?"

"Stop complaining," Wanda said. She enlarged the seam in the bubble, using the loop again. "Go on."

Dan lumbered out of the seam, still grumbling. Slowly he poked into the crevice. The last thing we saw was his eyes, real wide and white. Then he disappeared.

I held my breath and Frick fidgeted. Finally Dan waddled out, a lot faster than he went in. His flippers were loaded with what looked like trash. He climbed back in our bubble and shook water over us like a dog drying off, but the rest of the ocean stayed outside.

"Gone," he sniffed when he got back in our bubble dripping wet. "Doesn't look like he's been there in a while. But the cave is filled with this stuff."

There were lots of candy wrappers and empty bags. And there were whole bags of chocolate kisses and marshmallow peanuts that hadn't been opened. Wanda took an armful and said with a very sad expression, "That's *all?*"

"Hmmmf," Dan said, "and this note."

She took it eagerly. It was written in blue ink in a language that looked like Chinese with hiccups. "Dear Wanda," she read, "Sorry I had to give you the slip that way. Life is so boring on Antares XI. And there is no candy at all. You might as well relax—you won't find me. I'm just taking a little vacation. I'll be around to see you when the fun's over and I'm ready to go home."

Wanda slumped. Dan started grumbling about being brought on wild-goose chases. Stan said something in a sad slow growl and swam away.

"I'm sorry," Wanda said. "I brought everyone out here for nothing."

"That's not true," I heard myself saying "Frick and I never walked under the sea before. Besides, we'll help you find Edgar. We've got plenty of clues. Let's take all this stuff back to your house and study it."

I hated myself for saying that. What kind of a clue was a

bunch of candy wrappers? But it seemed to cheer Wanda a bit, and it kept Dan quiet. Frick was really enthusiastic about helping to find Edgar. He started suggesting all kinds of useless schemes on the way back.

"And we could put some candy out," he bubbled, "and paint it with luminous paint, and then follow the drips . . ."

I looked to see why he'd shut up. He was looking straight up. I followed his gaze and spotted a squid arm on a hook. There were lots of them right over us, and farther up, a big shadow on the surface. A boat.

"I bet it's the *Neptune Queen,*" he said.

We took a few more steps, then Frick got this devilish twinkle in his eyes. He was planning something.

"Wanda," he said suddenly, "could you make a private bubble just for me?"

"Why, yes," she replied, like she had been thinking of something faraway.

"Would you?" he pleaded.

Wanda looked at me. I shrugged. "If you don't," I said, "he'll just pester you to death. He's planning something silly."

Frick hopped up and down as Wanda made a seam in the bubble, then blew another bubble around him. Just before it closed, he snatched a bag of marshmallow peanuts from Dan. He giggled and slipped out into the water. But he didn't stay on the bottom. He pushed upwards and floated up among the fishing lines. In a moment he was lost in the green haze above us.

I started sweating. "I shouldn't have let him do that," I said. "I'm supposed to keep an eye out for him."

Wanda looked at me helplessly. For a moment I thought I was going to have to go after him. My heart started its tom-tomming again. But just as I was about to ask Wanda to make me a bubble, he swam into view. He crawled into the protection of our bubble snickering. The bag of candy was gone.

"What did you do?" I asked suspiciously.

"Oh, nothing." He smirked.

I couldn't get anything else out of him. Wanda stopped me when I threatened to punch him. Dan complained about being in such tight quarters with warring pups. So I shut up.

It was quiet on the way back. Frick would get excited over some sight or other, but other than that everyone was silent. Even Dan stopped grumbling. I think everyone had noticed how sad Wanda was. All the smile lines in her face had sort of wilted. Her blue eyes looked tired.

When we got back to the beach it had finished raining. Everything was gray and soggy. We went home with Wanda and shared some tea that Bob had brewed. Dan traveled home by refrigerator. I tried to cheer things up, and I guess I got too loud and obvious. It didn't do any good. We left, promising that we'd find Edgar before we went home Sunday. Secretly, I didn't think there was much hope of that. What could we do that a space ranger and her pygmy rhino couldn't?

I actually got to swim some that afternoon. But the memory of that shark kept me in the shallows.

Dad got home around sunset. A car loaded with a bunch of his friends let him off. I could tell by his expression this trip hadn't gone much better than the first. Boy, he was grumpy. And when Frick bounded out of the cottage with a forty-foot grin on his face, I began to smell a rat.

As Dad got his gear out of the back of their car, one of the men yelled, "Maybe you'd better take the kid with you from now on, Sweet Tooth Sam."

"Yeah," laughed another. "He can catch supper, and you can catch dessert."

Dad kicked the car. Frick was rolling in the sand with laughter. Now I knew what he had done with that bag of marshmallow peanuts. What a brat.

9: Duties and Disappointments

I had my beach towel, my sunglasses, tanning lotion, and diving mask all ready when Mr. Poole drove into our yard. He had an old riding lawn mower in the back of his truck. I had forgotten all about my promise to make a float for Poole's Hardware! There went my day on the beach.

"Howdy, Jenny." He smiled. "Sorry I haven't been able to get this to you before now. I was real busy."

"I've been sort of occupied myself," I said, trying not to sound disappointed he was here.

"Spent all day yesterday helping Mr. Hall clean up his place," Mr. Poole chatted. "Somebody made off with two whole boxes of chocolate almond bars. Never seen anything like it before."

"That's awful," I said. It sounded like Edgar had been busy, too.

"Well, you think you can turn this into a prize-winning Poole's Hardware float?" He pointed at the rusty mower.

"I can try," I gulped. I regretted ever saying I would.

Mr. Poole left some tools and some cardboard boxes and some spray paint for us to use on the float. It was already Thursday. That left only Friday to work on it before the parade Saturday. I decided we'd better get started. Back went all the beach stuff.

Frick wasn't much help. He kept trying to sneak off and I had to keep threatening him.

"But we promised to help Wanda find Edgar," he whined.

"I know. But we promised Mr. Poole first. Hand me that pair of scissors, and stop whining."

Wanda stopped by before she went searching. She was riding the bicycle with the bahoogie tires. Her face was still sad. Ordinarily, her expression was peaceful. But today she only looked tired and sleepy.

"I intend to search the woods today," she said.

I told her what Mr. Poole had said about the missing chocolate. "That means Edgar would be closer to town, doesn't it?" I said.

She seemed to shrug. "Perhaps. But it would be difficult for him to hide. I think he might be living elsewhere and coming into town for raids at night." She looked off toward Tomochee National Forest.

For a moment, I almost forgot about the float. Wanda looked so lost and lonely. But she got on her bicycle and was gone before I could say anything.

"Poor Wanda," Frick said. "I wish there was something we could do to help her."

I sighed and eyed the clunky old lawn mower we were trying to turn into a float. "We can't help Wanda. We can't even do what we have to do. I wish she could help *us*."

I was sure Wanda could come up with some of her "magic" to make the float look like something special. But I didn't have the heart to ask her that. Especially not now. We would just have to make this magic on our own.

We worked until we couldn't stand the sight of cardboard. I had finally decided on a theme, and we cut out cogs and springs and stuff. Later, I would spray the whole thing to look like metal. It was supposed to be a big hardware machine, with lots of screws and stuff that you could find at Poole's Hardware. It looked like a bunch of ripped up cardboard.

It was after lunch before we hit the beach.

The rain hit the beach about ten minutes after we did. I didn't even have a chance to jump in the water, and I still came home soaking. It was one of those tropical rainstorms. Mom invented inside games for us to play, but I still felt down.

Supper was nice. Mom fixed the rest of Frick's fish, with a special sauce of hers, and it was great. I think it gave Dad indigestion, though. He wasn't having such a great vacation either.

We were supposed to take the telescope out again, but Dad didn't feel like it, which was a shame because the rain had cleaned up the sky. The stars were bright. He let us visit Wanda instead.

Her wide smile was there again to greet us. Bob was brewing tea.

"Any luck?" I said hopefully.

She seemed to sag as she sat down. The smile faded. She made an odd gesture, pressed her palm against her nose. "No. Edgar's really given me the slip this time. He must have planned this for months."

"This time?" Frick squeaked. "You mean he's escaped Antares XI before?"

"Oh, yes. He didn't get very far that time. He was discovered in the water supply of a tourist ship. They could taste him."

Bob brought in the tea and poured everyone a cup. There were cookies, too. Bob sat across from us and opened himself a beer.

"Well, then," I said, "it seems like someone should have been watching Edgar, if he had tried before."

Bob honked and shot me a dirty glance. Wanda sighed. "He was my responsibility. After the first time, headquarters was going to ship him far from any spaceport. But I knew Edgar would hate that, so I had him placed under my custody. That's why there are no other rangers with me to search. I have to find him myself. With Bob's help, of course."

I felt like an idiot. I had only made her feel worse.

"What's that?" Frick said suddenly. He was looking at the TV.

It was a very old model. It looked like an old radio in a wood cabinet. It had a small screen. In the center of the screen was this orange spark, glowing bigger, then smaller.

"Oh," said Wanda, struggling to get up. "It's Mom!"

Bob stood up quickly and saluted, trying to hold the beer behind his back. Wanda ran to the TV set and turned it on. Frick and I both stood at attention. It looked like something important.

A lady appeared on the screen. She looked a lot like Wanda, only she had a purple suit on and a weird black hat. Behind her was some kind of map. She made the same kind of salute Bob had, wiggling her fingers underneath her chin.

"Fraznoogle Quap!" Wanda said.

"Grikkle daliki zort," replied Mom.

It went on like that. The woman on the screen asked several questions, and Wanda replied in the same language. Then the woman seemed to get kind of upset. She said something in several short sentences and pointed to a blue box on her desk. The screen went dark.

"What did your mother say?" Frick puzzled.

Wanda tried to smile. "She's not my mother. She's my Mother Superior. We just call her Mom. She's in charge of this quadrant of the galaxy. She was telling me I've only got two more days before my mission is up."

Bob muttered something (I don't think it was a compliment to Mom) and took another drink of beer.

I wasn't sure what it would mean if Wanda didn't find Edgar. Probably disgrace for a witch. But before I could say anything, Wanda turned to me.

"How was your day?" she asked. "I'm afraid I'm caught up too much in my own problems. I saw you trying to repair that conveyance down in front of your dwelling."

"Huh?" said Frick.

"That was no conveyance," I said. "That was a float. Or it's going to be a float when we're finished."

Wanda quirked an eyebrow. "You intend to take it to sea?"

I laughed. "No. I don't know why they call it a float. It's just a thing that moves, with decorations on it. We promised to make one for Mr. Poole for the Crab Trap Festival."

Suddenly a funny light flickered in her eyes. "Festival?" she said.

"Yeah," Frick said. "Every year this time. They have a big parade and a barbecue. It's to celebrate crabs. Lots of people and rides and cotton candy."

Wanda's smile suddenly ignited again. "That's it!" she whooped. Bob nearly dropped his beer. "Edgar loves parades and crowds and candy! I knew there was some reason for him coming here!"

Even Bob's eyes sparkled. "Yeah," he growled. "Remember the note? He said he'd see you when the fun was over!"

"He'll be there, all right," Wanda said. "At the parade!"

"But how?" I said. "Where's a giant crab going to hide?"

"Oh, he'll find a place. He's been planning this. He may be disguised as a tree or a bush, but he'll be hiding somewhere around town."

"Maybe we could go into town with you tomorrow and hunt for him," Frick suggested.

"Not us," I frowned. "We have to finish Mr. Poole's float."

"That's quite all right," Wanda sighed. "Now that I know his whereabouts, I can use the detection unit." She smiled again. "Wouldn't Mom be surprised if I brought Edgar in early!"

I felt better as we left Wanda's house. Even if we couldn't help her look for Edgar tomorrow, we seemed to have helped. Frick was terribly disappointed that I was holding him to his promise to help me build the float. He was sure he could find Edgar.

We finished the float the next day. It was big and square and had all sorts of gears and cogs and things on it. We spray painted it to look like aluminum. It wasn't as neat as I had pictured it. I was worried about the cogs coming off on the long ride to town. It was no prize winner, but it would have to do.

Just as we finished, I spotted Wanda cycling back from town. We waved and ran out to meet her, but halfway there I could tell she had failed. She was sweaty and dusty. She held what looked like a transistor radio with a long antenna in one hand.

"Is that the detector?" Frick asked.

She nodded. "It makes a noise when I point it at what I'm looking for. It's tuned for borxnees. I think I aimed at every tree or bush in Cobb's Cove. Anything that was about as high as a borxnee." She shrugged sadly. "Nothing."

"Look," I said, licking my lips, "we have to be in the parade tomorrow morning. But after that, we can help you look for Edgar. Maybe he's hiding on top of buildings. Maybe he's hiding in the town water tank. We can find him."

"Thank you," she said slowly. "I'll look for you after the parade, then."

But before she could leave, Frick said, "Hey, what's all the Wooster sauce for?"

I hadn't noticed the box in Wanda's bicycle basket before. It was a crate of Worcestershire sauce, unopened. "Oh, just something for the trip home." She smiled mysteriously. "I picked it up while I was in town."

She was gone before I could ask her what she could possibly use so much for.

That night, before we went to bed, I found Frick looking out the bedroom window. Wanda and Bob were out on the dunes, prowling. She was singing her song and Bob was kicking up billows of sand. The sky was cloudy. They were just outlines.

"You know," Frick said softly, "I think I liked Wanda better when she was a witch. Now she's just an alien with problems like everyone else. Witches are more fun."

I didn't even point out that she was still just as much a witch as ever. It was just Frick's image of her that had changed. My respect for Alice and her law went up some more.

10: The Clockwork Crab of Cobb's Cove

I looked at the Poole's Hardware float. It lay up to its axles in hot sand, hopelessly bogged down beside the road. Frick was sniffing back tears.

"What are we gonna do, Jenny?" he wailed.

I looked around like I expected to see a wrecker coming or something. The cottage was wiggling in the heat, distant and empty. A hundred meters away was the highway, wiggling in the heat also. Flashes of cars went past. I shrugged. "I dunno," I said.

"But there's nobody here!" he howled. "Mom and Dad are already at the festival. And so is Wanda!"

I wanted to punch Frick. Mom and Dad had gone ahead, since the float wouldn't fit in the back of the car. And we had both seen Wanda off to search for Edgar in town. It wasn't going to do any good to howl about it.

"What are we going to do, Jenny?"

I was thinking. And trying not to kick myself for driving into the soft sand. We could have gone back to the cottage and called Mr. Poole, but it was locked now. And Wanda had mentioned that Bob was visiting some relatives (through the refrigerator? I wondered) so I couldn't go to him for help.

What a miserable vacation. I felt awful. Not only was Wanda failing, but I had just guaranteed we would, too. Poor Mr. Poole would have no float. I wanted to cry too, but I had to show Frick how to be strong.

"There's nothing we can do," I finally said. It was the truth. "We just have to hope someone will stop and help us. Maybe somebody can pull the snicking thing out of the sand." I sounded like Dad.

The fourth car stopped. I guess we looked pretty pitiful. It was a bunch of tourists, out of state. They wore loud tropical shirts.

"Hi, kid," the driver said. "Going to town? Hop in."

"Uh, could you help us get our float out of the sand, sir?" I said.

He leaned around us and spotted the nearly buried float. It looked like a fallen satellite. He made a pained face and shook his head.

"Look, kid, we're late for the festival, and I don't have any rope or chains or stuff like that. I'll be glad to give you a lift into town, though."

I gulped and said okay. It was probably the best choice, and I didn't want to turn down a ride. We tumbled in the back with the rest of the kids.

I stuffed the rolled-up banner for the float into my top pocket. The other kids were giggling at my overalls. I had borrowed them from Bob. I was supposed to be a mechanic when I drove the float. Now I just looked silly.

Frick was recovering. "I guess we just tell Mr. Poole what happened."

"Yeah. He's real nice. He won't be mad."

Frick smiled. "Now we can help Wanda look for Edgar instead of being in the parade."

I was glad when we left the tourists. They had to park on the outskirts of town, and we lost them in the crowd. And what a crowd! I had never seen so many people in Cobweb Cove, not even at festivals. They were packed together like matches.

Balloons and streamers were everywhere. People were blowing paper horns and yelling. And there was stuff to eat on almost every street corner. There was shrimp and crab legs and fish and hush puppies and barbecue and hot dogs, even pizza! And there was candy. Cotton candy machines seemed to have invaded the town. They were whipping out pink clouds. There were lots of candy apples, too, and peanut brittle and Popsicles.

"Let's eat!" Frick slobbered. I had to hold him back.

"Wait a minute. We've got to find Mr. Poole first and tell him not to look for his float!"

Frick looked heartbroken. I had to hang on to his collar every time we got near a candy seller. It was hard enough trying to squeeze through the crowd without Frick acting his age. And it was getting hotter, too.

Just then there was a sound like muffled thunder at the other end of town. Horns blared. Then something crashed like a tin shed falling into a hardware store. The crowd quieted to a dull roar. The parade was beginning. A brass band was assaulting the street.

It got even harder to push our way, with everyone straining to see. We came to the circle where all the shops are just as the first marching band did. It was deafening. A white flag with yellow tassles passed by over people's heads. It had a crab on it and a Neptune's fork too. Everyone cheered.

Frick could squeeze better than me, and he got to Poole's first. I found him staring at the CLOSED sign on the door.

"Of course," I moaned. "Mr. Poole will be watching the parade too."

"We'll never find him in all this," Frick whined.

"That's what I've been saying," a familiar voice sounded behind us. It was Wanda. She looked weary and about as discouraged as we. Her normally crisp hair was sagging on her moist forehead. And she was carrying about a hundred cotton candies. But she grinned at us.

"Wanda!" Frick whooped. "Our float got stuck, so now we can help you look for Edgar!"

Wanda was overjoyed. "Good." She giggled. "You're perfect—Edgar won't suspect you at all! I've been wandering around trying to lure him out with candy, but he knows me."

"Do you think he would come out with all these people around?" Frick hollered over the crowd.

"Oh, Edgar loves people. But I just want to find out where he is and keep an eye on him. There would be a panic if he came out now. Here, you each take an armful of candy."

She dumped a cloud of cotton candy on each of us. I sputtered, "But . . ." We really ought to try to find Mr. Poole. But it seemed so impossible. Nearly as impossible as trying to find Edgar.

"Now." Wanda smiled. "You must hang around all suspicious bushes or objects that might be a giant crab hiding. He might be anywhere. If he goes for your candy, find me quickly and I'll put a homer signal on him. Good luck!"

She disappeared in the crowd before I could ask her what an object that might be a giant crab looked like. I looked hopelessly at Frick, who seemed to think it would be easy.

"You go look in the shrubbery in front of the library," he said around a happy mouthful of cotton candy. "I'll go across the street and hang around all the big rocks at the courthouse."

He was gone before I could tell him what a dumb idea that was. I wondered how I got into these situations and tried to shove my way to the town library. It seemed like all I had done on my spring vacation was work.

The Neptune County Library is a big white building with columns and about a thousand steps going to the door. It has shrubbery all around it and big oak trees on each side. Most of the steps and a lot of the tree limbs were covered with people when I got there, all watching the parade. I stopped for a minute and watched, too.

It was a better parade than last year. The floats looked better. There was one shaped like a shrimp boat with real nets all over it, and Miss Neptune rode in a float shaped like a seashell. She wore a bathing suit that ended in a tail so she looked like a mermaid. It almost made me feel better about getting our float stuck. We sure wouldn't have been much competition.

Then I remembered Edgar. Where could a giant crab hide around here? I pushed my way around back of the library where they keep a lot of old stuff. Old fire trucks and antique wagons—things like that. I offered a rusty boiler some cotton candy, but nothing moved.

I shinnied up a rain pipe and looked on the roof of the library. Nothing. I scanned the other rooftops from there, but no luck. I poked cotton candy into sewer gratings and over the tops of cisterns. I even climbed a fence at the monument works and offered some to a huge tombstone with angels all over it. Nothing.

I was about to go back around front of the library again when Frick ran up. At first I thought he'd found something.

"Have you got fifty cents?" he said. "I need some more cotton candy."

"I bet you do," I said, digging for money. "If you keep eating that stuff that way, you're gonna get sick."

"I didn't eat that much!" he protested. "I guess I dropped some."

"Any sign of Edgar?"

"Nope. I looked around the big rocks and the cannon, and up in the steeple. And under the stairs."

I told him to keep looking and not to eat the bait. He went back to the courthouse and I went around to explore the shrubbery.

There was a lot of it, too. Nobody noticed me because everyone was watching the parade. Another marching band was thundering by. It was dark in the maze of bushes. I found where they kept the library lawn mower, in a cubby underneath the stairs. But there were only spiders and some empty spray cans and old boxes. Nothing wanted candy there.

The other side of the stairs was just as jungly. The cotton candy was beginning to get bugs in it. Then I spotted something.

It was a big claw, half hidden in the tall grass next to the building. I froze. It gleamed dully. There were some more legs beside it.

"Edgar," I whispered.

Suddenly, I didn't want to poke any more cotton candy into dark corners. My heart was keeping time to a passing band. I had to find Wanda. I began backing out. Then I stepped on something hard. I looked down, then picked it up. It was a long bronze rod. It looked just like an antenna from a lobster, kind of prickly. I looked back at Edgar, but he still wasn't moving. At all.

Then, while I watched, one of the legs fell right over. It rattled. That wasn't Edgar! After inspection, it turned out to be some old hollow bronze lobster legs from the Neptune statue. There was a lobster body lying beside them. This must be where they put parts of the old statue that fall off. I sure felt silly.

Frick came back for more money. I yelled at him. He was almost crying, and swore that he hadn't eaten it all. He said it must be evaporating in the heat. I gave him my last fifty cents anyway.

Then I climbed up the library steps and sat down. I was

tired of looking for a giant crab. I was tired of working on my vacation. I watched the parade.

From where I was sitting I could see Frick across the street. He was watching the parade, too. He was probably tired of looking, like me. He was standing up on the base of the King Neptune statue. I couldn't see much of the statue because of a tree growing in front of it. He was taking little nibbles of cotton candy. I snorted. Wasn't eating it, huh?

Then I noticed something. I sat up. Suddenly I began noticing a lot of other things, some of which I'd already forgotten. They made a little ball of questions in my mind.

Frick was nibbling off the bottom of his cotton candy, like he always does. Then why was the top of the paper tube sticking way up over the pink fluff, like something had been eating from the top? Why would the city hide old broken pieces of statue instead of throwing them away or replacing them? And why were there empty cans of copper spray paint in the library storeroom? Wasn't that the kind of spray paint stolen from Mr. Poole? And now that I thought of it, weren't those empty *candy* boxes the spray paint cans had been in?

Suddenly, a light went on in my head. My heart started hammering again.

Then, *I saw it!* Something nipped down from behind the tree blocking my view. A shred of Frick's cotton candy disappeared. The something had looked just like a piece of statue!

I crossed the street between a band and the local dune buggy club, running all the way. Frick looked surprised to see me. He tried to lick the pink fringe of candy from around his lips.

"I know where Edgar is," I whispered as softly as I could over the sound of the band.

"Where?"

"Right above you. Don't look! Then he'll know we've seen him!"

Frick's eyes got real big.

"He's painted himself. He's coming out of Neptune's shell like all the other seafood. He's been there the whole time. Eating your cotton candy, too!"

Just then we both saw something flash away from the top of his candy. More was gone.

Frick gulped. I could hear it over the parade. "What are we gonna do, Jenny?"

My mind raced. "I've got to find Wanda, first of all. She'll know what to do. You stay here and make sure he's got enough candy."

Frick's eyes got even bigger. He swallowed bravely and looked up at the giant claws just over our heads. Most of Edgar was visible from where we stood, if you knew what to look for. The eyes gave him away. Everything else was bronzey, but his eyes were like bowling balls. They were looking at us.

Frick smiled nervously and took a half step toward the statue. He held out the ball of cotton candy. Just as timidly, Edgar extended a claw. It was weird. It looked just like the statue was moving, like it was mechanical. He took some candy. Frick giggled and moved a little closer.

I watched, amazed, as Frick made friends with Edgar. The big crab finally moved down almost to the bottom of the statue to get the rest of the goodies. And no one but me had noticed. Everybody else was cheering the parade.

But just as I turned to go, a freckled kid ran up to me. He had something in his hand. "Hey, watch that kid." He snickered. Before I could stop him, he lit a fuse on something and tossed it Frick's way.

BLAM! The firecracker went off. Frick squealed and jumped up in the air. Edgar lost his grip and tumbled off the statue! Suddenly Frick landed, straddling one of

Edgar's claws and hung on for dear life. Edgar's antennas were wiggling like crazy. I remembered Wanda saying he was afraid of loud noises.

I turned back to the freckled kid, but he hadn't seen Edgar. He was busy lighting another bomb.

"NO!" I hollered. But it was too late.

POW! A real big one exploded right under Edgar! Just like in the film, Edgar shot into the air. He and Frick sailed right over the heads of the crowd. A flying crab! They landed in the middle of the street, in a space between floats.

The band screeched to a halt. The crowd shut up. Eyes grew bigger all around the circle. I could feel the panic growing.

Edgar stumbled forward, unsure of what to do. Frick hung on.

Suddenly, inspiration hit me right between the eyes. I found myself in the street.

"Here, grab this!" I threw Frick the Poole's Hardware banner from my top pocket. He grabbed it. I stuck all of my cotton candy and caramel apples in the back pockets of the overalls and backed up under Edgar's nose.

"Ladies and gentlemen!" My voice kind of wobbled, but I continued. "In honor of Cobb's Cove's Crab Trap Festival, Poole's Hardware proudly presents . . . THE CLOCK-WORK CRAB!"

I extended my palm to Edgar and grinned. Blank eyes surrounded me. Then Frick caught on and unwound the banner. The Poole's Hardware sign fluttered in the breeze.

I felt the tug on my back pocket I'd been praying for, and started forward. Edgar followed, nibbling on the goodies.

Slowly, the band started up again. The float in front of us began moving. We were in the parade after all!

You could almost hear a click as the adults surrounding

us found an acceptable category to put Edgar in. He was a float! A walking clockwork model! Scattered clapping rolled around the circle until it became a wave of applause, then cheers. I'm sure it was as much from relief as enjoyment. Everyone was grinning. How happy they were that they didn't have to believe there was any such thing as a giant candy-eating crab! A couple of clever kids had almost made them believe the impossible. But Alice's Law triumphed.

I grinned as we paraded Edgar around under the town's noses.

When we rounded the circle I led Edgar waddling down a side street instead of going on with the parade. I ran. Edgar ran. Frick bobbed.

Finally, we were away from the crowds. I turned around to find Edgar crunching happily on a candy apple that was stuck to the seat of my pants.

"We did it!" Frick whooped.

I whooped too. I figured it was time for it. Then I turned to Edgar. "Listen, Edgar," I said sternly. "You've got to come along peacefully, now. It'll be better for you if you don't put up any resistance, you know."

The little fingerlike things around Edgar's mouth whirred. He said something to me in a high buzzing voice that I didn't catch. Then he headed for me.

I screamed.

Actually, all he did was snatch me up with his free claw and put me on his back, but I thought I was a goner. Then he headed straight for Summer Island. I didn't know a crab could run that fast, frontways. We didn't even bounce around much.

"I guess he's giving himself up." Frick shrugged.

Somebody from Iowa who drives a blue station wagon sure had an interesting vacation. I know because they were the only ones we met on the highway. They ran over a trash can and a ditch trying to get away from Edgar, when all they had to do was pass.

Right after that Wanda caught up with us on her bicycle. She was grinning a smile that made all her others look mild. People from Hecate must have more teeth than we do.

I know they have more legs. At least two more unfolded from that floppy dress, with webbed toes. They and the other two were pumping the bahoogie bicycle as fast as Edgar could run, which was fast.

We turned onto our drive. Bob was on top of a sand dune, hopping up and down to see Edgar.

We all hollered. I think even Edgar hollered. But I can't be sure.

11: A Meteor in Reverse

WE won the fifty dollar prize for the Most Original Float at the festival. There was a ceremony, with the mayor and everything. Of course they had to come out to the island, where Edgar carried us. They figured that's where we'd be. Everybody wanted to see the crab, but we explained the tragedy to them. I told them the spring that powered Edgar was wound too tight, and when we got to the beach, well ... he just kept right on going. There were his footprints (thanks to Wanda) leading straight into the surf. We were heartbroken about it. I think Frick even sniffled some, the little ham.

I've never seen Dad so happy. He called me a smart devil for keeping Edgar a secret from him. We told him Wanda had let us build it at her house, and she helped with the mechanics.

"See how wrong you were about her," Dad said. We just laughed.

It was sunset before the mayor and everyone left. Dad and Mom got to talking with some of their friends who'd stayed, so we had a chance to sneak off.

Wanda's grin hadn't left her. "Come in, come in. Tea and cookies for the detectives?" she bubbled.

I tried not to think of those two other legs under her dress and sampled the newest bag of cookies. I got a walrus.

"What's wrong with him?" Frick said. Edgar was in the corner with a huge ice bag on his shell. Most of the copper paint was scrubbed off. As we watched, he gave a kind of lurching hiccup.

"Oh, poor Edgar," Wanda said. "He's quite ready to go back home to Antares XI."

"He is?" I wondered.

"Yes. He only wanted a little vacation here, on the planet of his childhood, so he came for the festival. And after a diet of candy for a week, he'll be happy to get home to a steaming bowl of garnichy. Eh, Edgar?"

Edgar belched.

"So clever." She sighed. "Imagine, us looking all over and him in plain sight all along." She turned to us. "By the way, on behalf of the Ecological Relocation Service of Hecate, I would like to present you with something for your help. I'm sure I would never have found Edgar without you."

We protested, but she gave it to us anyway. It was a purple book with *very* weird white writing in it. Well, sort of a book. It was round like a record with a hole in the center. It fit on a stand, and you could flip each page up in a funnel shape and spin the book around to read. I know it sounds weird, but it worked anyway. It had pictures of all kinds of animals in it, some of which looked familiar.

"Our catalog," Wanda said proudly. "A field guide to relocated or pending species."

"Wow, thanks," Frick stuttered.

Just then I noticed what Bob was doing. As usual, he had been going about his business quietly while everyone else was talking. He had another pair of overalls on, and he was pouring Worcestershire sauce down the kitchen drain. Bottle after bottle.

"What is he doing?" I gawked.

"Oh. Bob is refueling for the flight back. He's the engineer, you know."

Bob looked over his shoulder and smiled humbly.

ALIENS OF THE WORLD

"We have a long way to go tonight," Wanda concluded.

I was confused. "I've been meaning to ask you, where is your ship?"

Frick giggled. "You don't know by *now?*"

Wanda smiled and gestured proudly. "It's all around us. A class X-35 Starcruiser built in the form of an Earth dwelling. It should have been updated, of course. It was designed a hundred of your years ago, but there wasn't time to adapt it when Edgar escaped."

"Remember the burnt shells?" Frick coaxed. "And the melted mud? And all that fog last Friday night when we got here? Steam."

Wanda nodded thoughtfully and sipped her tea. "Yes, the burners get quite hot."

"Then," I gulped, "you *were* that long meteor we saw."

"The house was," Frick corrected.

"And it runs on *Worcestershire sauce?*" I coughed.

"Well," Wanda shrugged, "we had to make it something that we could get easily here. We didn't have enough room to bring our own return fuel. The engines have been altered to accept it."

I blinked, trying to imagine a gas pump with a squirt nozzle.

"I need the key to activate the framisglottis, Wanda," Bob grumbled.

She unhooked something from her belt and handed it to him. He inserted it beside the faucet in the sink and turned the hot water handle. No water came out, but the house rattled.

"The magic medal!" Frick stared.

"Yes," she said. "It's the ignition key and the key to the stellar batteries. That was why I was so happy you found it. Without it we'd be stuck here. You two really have been a help."

Just then the kitchen buzzer went off again. It was Edgar

who jumped behind the sofa this time, though.

"We have five minutes to lift-off," Bob announced. He was reading the dials on the stove and adjusting a blender.

"Oh, dear." Wanda sighed. "Partings seem so final. It has been such a joy to know you both. And a pleasure to work with you. I'll mention you in my report to Mom."

We shook hands with her.

She walked us to the pier. When we were on land, she clanged the old ship's bell nailed to the mailbox twice. The pier groaned, the ropes tightened and then the whole thing folded right up. Click, click, click the boards rolled up and fastened to the porch. She waved one last time and went inside.

We held our breaths. The weathercock on the roof rotated as if feeling for a course between the stars. Three . . . two . . . one!

It wasn't loud. Just a dull rumbling that might have been distant thunder. And a lot of steam as the house lurched up into the air. It floated away over the dunes. Soon it was a point of light, and getting smaller.

Frick sighed. "I still think she's a Sand Witch."

At that moment, I was inclined to agree with him. With the new old house gone, the whole week seemed like a spell. At least we had the catalog to keep.

We walked back over the dunes without talking. When we got near our cottage, Frick pointed. "There's Dad."

He had the telescope set up. He waved us over.

"Would you kids like to look at the Great Globular Cluster in Hercules?" he said.

We had seen it before. It's just a fuzzy thing, real dim. But we both acted interested 'cause Dad expects it. He turned to look for the right constellation. Then he acted excited.

"Look!" he pointed. "A shooting star!"

We looked up. It was a bright streak, and it only lasted a

minute. It was in the direction of the constellation Hydra. But it was going up, not coming down. I grinned and elbowed Frick.

Dad paused, then dropped his hand. He looked back at his telescope quickly. "Must have been a high jet," he muttered.

Frick and I glanced at each other and broke into laughter. Wait till I tell Alice!